CATCHING MEMORIES

CARL GREGORY

ISBN: 9798218473914

CONTENTS

For My Father, John D.

They want to ask you, do you remember?
But they're afraid of what you might say,
It was your lifetime; they were your memories,
Can they be somewhere, safely locked away?
When memories fly, where do they go?
To some place safe, they need to know,
For if they're forgotten, and gone from your mind,
Then what were the years worth,
If you've left them behind?

Carl Gregory
"When Memories Fly"

CATCHING MEMORIES

CHAPTER 1

Snakes

Five-year-old Blake Eaton lay in a field of grass and wildflowers, watching yellow butterflies and metallic green mosquito hawks flying in the hot air. He wasn't aware of the fat rattlesnake a mere foot behind him, coiled and ready to strike; the noise of cicadas and bumblebees muffled the buzzing of its tail.

He heard his father say, as clear as if he lay beside him, and not carried on the breeze, or imagined, "Lunch is ready, son. Come inside now." Blake stood and ran to the big white house in the distance, leaving the snake behind. The animal uncoiled and slithered away into the warm, open meadow; its guard duty was done.

Thirty years later, Blake sat at his parent's kitchen table eating food he'd brought from the fish and chips drive-through, and his father repeated a question for the fifth or sixth time. Blake's mother, not trying to conceal her irritation, raised her voice and said, "James, you've asked him that, and he's answered you. He said yes, he's still drawing pictures.

Now eat your lunch."

"I need a shovel, Mary," he said.

Blake took a spoon from a drawer and handed it to his father.

"Now, that's not a shovel. That's a fork," he said.

"That's right, Dad, but don't worry about it. It doesn't matter what you call it as long as it works."

"James, you know it's a spoon," Mary said. "Sometimes I wonder if he says things like that just to get me upset." His dad bowed his head and glanced at Blake with a look of devilment in his eyes, and grinned. They played this wicked game with Mary; James loved getting a rise out of his wife, and Blake enjoyed being his accomplice.

The men shared much the same sense of humor, and Blake looked like his handsome father, but that's where the similarities ended. Blake had finer features, blonde hair, and green eyes; his father's hair had turned gray, and his icy blue eyes caused people to stare. His mother was known for her beauty and auburn hair, and the years had been kind to both.

James loved hunting, horses, and being a good parent, and in his youth was known to be a ladies' man. Blake was artistic and musical, and, while perusing photos of Greek sculptures in his mother's art book, realized he was different from other boys in a way he didn't yet understand.

He'd kept his sexual proclivities a secret until he graduated from high school, and when he finally told his parents, it was so anticlimactic he thought they might not have heard him. He stood in the kitchen watching his mother wash the breakfast dishes. His heart began to beat heavily, his palms began to sweat, and he thought he might faint.

"There's something I want to tell you," Blake said, "and you, too, Dad." His father, engrossed in his newspaper, looked at him with a concerned expression as his glasses slid slowly down his nose. Blake had never been in any trouble, and this sounded serious.

His mother said, "Well, what is it, son? You know you

can tell us anything." She, too, was worried by Blake's appearance and the flush of his skin. Blake took a deep breath and grabbed the back of a dining chair, using it for support in case he got the vapors and fell.

"Well, the thing is," he exhaled and said, "it seems I'm gay." Mary looked at her husband, who returned to his newspaper.

"It seems?" She laughed and said, "You think you've been keeping that a secret all this time?" She giggled softly and returned to her dishes.

James dropped the newspaper a few inches and said, "You're too handsome not to be a little bit queer." Blake looked at his feet.

"Hold your head up, son. Be proud of yourself. We are."

Blake walked into the field around his parents' home and cried. The relief was overwhelming. He had told his darkest secret to them and felt stupid he thought they hadn't known. Now, no one else mattered; he could tell the world.

He dried his eyes and went back inside; Mary was still complaining to James about things he couldn't help doing. He knew his parents loved each other, and his mother was in denial about his father's disease and what the future held for them. She often admonished him about something trivial; it was part of their love dynamic, and continuing to do so as long as she could comforted his mother. James was amiable and adept at letting things roll off his back, and was glad to be her perfect foil.

"What's going to happen when one day you think I'm a horse or something?" she said, shaking her head at her French fries.

"Well, Mary, I guess I'll saddle you up and ride you to town," James said, laughing the way he used to before his dementia took hold.

"Well, I wish you wouldn't act that way. What are people going to say?" She looked at Blake and said, "Just yesterday, he took a leftover baked potato and cut it up into little pieces. Why? I don't know, but I wanted to eat that potato, and it made me mad."

"She yelled at me like I'd cut off her foot or something," James said, turning to Blake and giving him a secret wink.

"See, you remember that!" she said. "Well, why did you do that, James? I wanted that potato, and you got up and cut it into little pieces, then let it sit on the counter for me to clean up. A perfectly good potato!"

"Mother, he can't help it. Can't you understand that? Calm down, it was just a fu… a potato."

She began clearing the table. "I'm just afraid, Blake. What's going to happen to him? How am I going to deal with this?"

"You're doing your best, Mother, but pretty soon you'll need help."

"I know that, and I know he can't help it, but it seems like everyone takes his side and I'm the mean old woman that takes care of him. And don't you curse in my house." She sighed and stared at her husband. "You don't have any idea what it's like here all day with him wandering around. I never know what he's gonna do next. And he won't listen to me. He won't sit and watch TV; he's always got to be doing something. Some days I think I'll go bonkers. It's worse than having a kid around."

She glanced at Blake and continued. "Like the other night, he woke me up at two o'clock in the morning to tell me he was going to go paint the car. Paint the car! At two in the morning! I told him he couldn't do that, but he wouldn't listen, as usual, and got up and put his pants on backward, and went out to the garage. I had to get out of bed and follow him, and he's standing there staring at the shelves, with his rear end showing through the zipper. He looked at me with that silly grin he gets and said, 'My momma is out here, isn't she?' His mother! Dead for twenty years."

"Well, maybe she *was* out there, Mother. Who knows?"

"I doubt it. Mother Eaton never came here when she was alive. Why would she start now?"

Blake had very few memories of his family visiting his dad's mother, even though they lived in the same town. He suspected he saw her often, without Mary. It was obvious that the women didn't like each other.

Years ago, he asked his father why they didn't get along. He answered, "My mother wasn't quite as, well, liberal as Mary. She didn't agree with gay liberation, among other things. The Anita Bryant crap kind of brought it to a head; Mary told my mother what she thought of that bitch, and they barely spoke after that."

Blake answered, "Because of me, then."

"Well, yes. I was proud of your mother for that." Blake saw his mother a little differently from then on; suddenly, he felt closer to her.

Now, Mary was doing her best for her husband, and he wanted to help her if he could.

"Mother, I know it's hard on you. You need a break, and we need to start thinking about a place for..." Blake glanced at his father and said, "Never mind. We'll talk some other time."

"Did I ever tell you about Chief?" James asked. Mary sighed.

"Yes, Dad, you did, but I like hearing that story."

"He was a big palomino, yellow as gold, and I swear as shiny. Long, beautiful mane. People said he should have been in the movies. My daddy was friends with a Seminole Indian Chief who gave him to my daddy, then Daddy gave him to me. So I named him Chief. He was smart but got a little feisty sometimes. He loved to run me into the fence. But I taught him to jump logs, and we'd go hunting and sometimes stay out all night camping.

"One time we camped down near the river, fishing, and I stepped barefoot on a big old water moccasin. He must've been seven or eight feet long, I swear, and he bit me right in my skinny little calf and hung on with his fangs, and Chief broke his rope and ran over and stomped that snake to death. I got on Chief and he ran like hell to town, not to home. He took me to some people on the street, and they took me to the doctor's and he saved my leg. Chief knew where to go. He was one smart horse. The doc said if I'd gone home I would've died. Chief knew it. He loved me like I loved him."

"Whatever happened to him?" Blake knew the end of the story, but it was nice to hear his father remembering things and know there were still memories alive in him.

"My daddy had to sell him. My leg had just about healed from the snake bite, then Chief stepped in a little sink-hole and fell on me and broke my good leg. I couldn't walk on it for months, and Daddy decided that was a sign he should sell him. We were poor, and Momma needed things for the kids. Daddy got a good offer for Chief, so he let him go. That almost killed me. Some people down the road bought him, and a few times he ran away and spent the day with me before they came to take him back. The man who bought him moved away, and I never found out where to. Someone said they sold Chief but didn't know any more about it.

"We never saw Chief again, and I always wondered how he made out. I hope they took good care of him, like he did of me." His voice changed, and Blake saw he was trying not to cry; that happened a lot lately.

"That was a long time ago, Daddy."

"Yep, during the depression."

"I guess your family needed that horse money."

"The depression didn't bother us. We were poor to begin with, so it didn't change anything ; we kept on doing for ourselves like we always had and got by. There wasn't much money, but we were happy. Us kids worked in the garden growing vegetables, and we had chickens for eggs and meat. Sometimes Daddy would go in with the neighbors and buy a whole cow or pig to slaughter. We had a smokehouse and Daddy would cure hams, sausages, and smoke mullet, too. We'd go camping on the Gulf and fish for days.

"Did I ever tell you I almost killed myself jumping off the roof of the smokehouse? Almost broke my neck trying to fly. Ha!" James's eyes were fixed on a point of air in the middle of the room. "I'd forgotten about that; making butterfly wings out of a big cardboard box I found in somebody's trash. Maybe I was a little crazy. Don't know why I made them look like a butterfly, either; painted them bright colors. Always liked butterflies, but you'd think I would've made 'em like a crow's or a hawk's, me being a boy." He paused and looked into the space in front of him again, remembering.

"We were happy. I loved my parents, and they loved all eight of us, and all of us kids loved each other and looked out for each other. And we worked hard and did fine."

"You still work hard, Dad. You always did."

"Yep, I had to," he said, and Blake thought he caught a flicker of a memory in his eyes, perhaps a little sadness, or a fleeting vision of what his life might have been if he hadn't had to work so hard to support his wife and family in the way his wife longed to become accustomed. And, for a man who had to quit school in the eighth grade to go to work, he had done well. Blake was raised in a gracious home with a swimming pool; they drove new cars and wore stylish clothes, spent summers at the beach, and his mother had occasional household help.

James looked at Blake and said, "Did I ever tell you about my horse? The one named Chief?

Mary groaned.

CHAPTER 2

Up Into the Past

That's when Blake got the idea. "Dad, how would you like to find out what happened to Chief?"

"Oh, he's dead now," he said, looking at Blake as if his son were dumber than he realized.

"I know, but we could go there and find out who owned that farm and where they are now, and, I know it's kind of iffy, and a long shot, but if we talked to the right people, they might remember Chief."

"My momma's up there," he said.

"Well, we might see her, too."

Mary spoke up, "James, your mother's been dead a long time. She's not even buried there. They moved down here, don't you remember?"

"But if I visit the old house, it would be like seeing her and Daddy again."

"Well, I'll take a week off and we'll get in my car and drive up there and see what we can find out. I think the old thing will be up to the trip." Blake glanced at his mother, held his breath, and hoped he'd hear the answer he wanted. "Give you some time off, too."

"Oh, I'm not going. You can be sure of that." Blake exhaled. "That's too long a ride for me, and I care nothing about seeing that old place again. Although I wouldn't mind stopping off in Crossville to visit my momma's grave and spend some time with my sisters. But you don't want to take care of your dad by yourself for an entire week in motel rooms, do you?"

"Well, if it gets too bad, we'll come home again," he answered. "We'll do that, then; drop you off at Evelyn's on the way to Cedar Grove."

"But a whole week? Who'll take care of the house?"

"We can find somebody; ask Polly, next door. It'd only be a week." He was relieved. The drive to Crossville would take a few hours, but after that, he and his father would be free to explore his dad's memories without his mother intruding and correcting them. They could have a beer in a roadside cafe and smoke a cigar like men do, and cuss and tell dirty stories, and pee in the bushes on the side of the road; the things Blake had always envied in his friends' good times with their fathers. It seemed James had worked most of the days of Blake's childhood, but when he took some time off to go hunting or fishing with his brother, he thought better than to ask Blake to come along. Blake detested guns and hated catching fish; he had trouble forcing himself to impale a wiggling, living creature on a hook to be eaten alive.

Back in his home office, Blake sent out some jobs to clients with an out-of-office note attached, made some phone calls, wrote a couple of letters, and got enough information to begin the search. Amanda, his assistant, said, "Don't worry about the office while you're gone. I've got it covered. You need some time off. You've been kind of a grouch lately. Maybe you'll get laid."

"That's your answer to everything, isn't it?"

She laughed and said, "No, not everything. But it can't hurt. Have fun!"

"Don't forget to send the invoices. The account's looking a bit lean."

"Don't worry, I want to get paid."

A few days later, Blake packed his aging Impala and drove the interstate an hour to his parents' house. He loved his car, but it was far beyond its prime, and soon he'd have to give it up for something newer. He was sure it was up to the journey, and he wanted one more road trip in her to say goodbye, and the thought of parting with so much money for a new car depressed and worried him.

James was sitting in his wing-back chair, his suitcase beside him. Mary, still in the bathroom, called out that they should eat something, make sure Dad packed his medicine, throw some seed out for the birds, and put a new bulb in the porch light. James stared, unfocused, into the air in front of him, and Blake saw that today was not one of his good ones; he seemed agitated and worried, his fingers entwined and thumbs rubbing his palms.

"Dad, are you okay?"

James looked at him, puzzled, and said, "Where are you taking me? To Chattahoochee, to the nut house?"

"We're going up north to your old farm to find out what happened to Chief."

"Well, that's pretty crazy. Chief's been dead a long time, and I bet the old house isn't there anymore. This doesn't seem like a good idea to me. Who's going to take care of my wife?"

"She's coming with us, Dad. Don't worry. Everything's going to be fine. We're gonna have a good time. I'll bet the old house is just like you left it."

They drove out of town, joined the main highway and crossed the bridge that spanned the river flowing north to Jacksonville. It rose in the vast marshes beyond their town, on the distant horizon of tall grass and cloud mountains. James sat in the front seat looking out the window, remarking on things in the landscape he remembered: churches, old wooden buildings now silvered with age, big white birds perched on Brahman cattle in fields of wildflowers, an overgrown cemetery; things that were part of his past. Mary sat in the back seat reading a *House Beautiful* magazine, lost in photos of rooms she'd never inhabit.

"Blake, how come you never became an interior decorator like you wanted to?"

He had explained to her many times, "Designer, not decorator, Mother; there's a big difference."

"Well, we could have used either one in the family. Think of the discounts. You wouldn't believe what I had to pay for my new curtains." Mary turned a page and began to dream again.

They drove up into the past. The oak trees along the road seemed to be draped with more gray moss on them the farther north they traveled, until the railroad appeared alongside the highway. They were almost to the town where his mother had been born and raised, and where she'd met his father.

Mary was a teenager with her first summer job, working at the dime store. She was behind the counter, bending over a candy bin, when James walked in and saw her white pleated skirt showing more than it would normally allow. James was a leg man, and he had found a pair that fit his idea of perfection. Mary straightened up, smoothed her skirt, and asked if he needed help; James could see the rest of her was as pretty as her long limbs.

"Gimme a bag of those orange slices, please. The small bag."

James smiled at her and their hands touched as she handed him the brown paper sack, smiled back, and said, "That's a nickel." He asked her what time she got off work, and Mary, noting that the young man dressed well, was clean-shaven and very handsome, and, she being young and naïve, said, "Five o'clock".

He returned at closing time, and they walked to the little cafe across the street and had sweet tea in the sultry afternoon, and the rest is history. They got married a year later in Mary's fundamentalist church, then moved south to James's hometown. Soon, two children joined them: Blake first, and a few years later, his sister, Margaret.

James worked hard and took risks. He opened a little sundries store, then a grocery; after that, a restaurant, a barbecue grill, and a cocktail lounge. He began building houses that were affordable for almost anyone, especially since he held the mortgage on them. He kept buying and selling and soon became a wealthy man. Almost everyone liked and respected him, even the people of color who lived in a clearly defined part of town. James extended low-interest credit to them on everything from bananas to shotgun houses, and his customers seldom missed a payment because he was their friend.

Blake parked the car in Aunt Evelyn's driveway. The house was well-kept and inviting, and the pink stucco was still bright in the afternoon sun. Mary got out of the car and leaned in through the window to kiss James; Blake carried her suitcase up to the porch and placed it near the wide swing on chains where he'd spent many summer days as a young boy listening to the birds and reading in the hot, humid afternoons, the sound of distant thunder lulling him to sleep. Sometimes in the warm evenings, he'd sit there and listen to his mother and Aunt Evelyn singing "My Happiness" in close harmony. The smell of sun-warmed geraniums and the sight of Spanish moss draped in the gigantic oaks hurtled him into his murky and uncomfortable past. Blake said hello to his aunt, who seemed to have gone deaf since she only nodded to him without speaking, then turned to Mary and said, "Come on in. Does anybody need the little boy's room?"

She glanced at Blake, and he answered, "No thanks." His aunt didn't like him, and he felt the same about her. They could use the gas station up the road if James wanted the toilet, and he'd rather go there than have to endure his aunt's pursed lips and beady-eyed, judgmental stare. He could imagine her in the bathroom spraying the toilet seat with Lysol after he'd left it. He was relieved when they drove away, as he'd always been as a child.

The two men got back on the road and sped west toward Cedar Grove. Blake said, "Let's drive over to Gulfpoint and spend the night. We're not in any hurry."

James said, "Suits me," so they detoured down to the Gulf of Mexico and came to the little fishing village where they'd made so many happy memories. James's family had owned a cabin built on stilts over the water, but it was gone now, taken by a hurricane years ago. They found the spot where it had stood, and in their minds saw its unpainted clapboard reflecting like silver in the calm brown gulf water.

They drove in silence except for the crushed oyster shell road making its gritty, nostalgic crunch. Thoughts of those days brought them close, as if it had been only months, not years. Blake could taste fresh mullet and buttered grits and hush puppies, and smell the acerbic odor of kerosene lamps glowing on the poker table, and the pungent vinegar his mother rubbed on his sunburned skin. Dolphins swam in the channel off the back porch, and Blake loved throwing them fish from the bait box. Sometimes his dad would give him driving lessons in the new station wagon while he sat on his lap and James worked the pedals, or show him how to clean a fish and throw the offal to the screaming seagulls overhead.

The salt smells brought memories of times when they were happy and safe, with the family together, before things changed. They thought they would stay the same, but so much of what they loved had vanished. Between the hurricanes and the condominiums rising from the coral ground, little that mattered was left. The two men stared in silence at the space above the shallow gulf, empty now of everything except their memories.

James said, "Didn't I live here?"

Blake said, "Yes, Dad, long ago. We all lived here, together, in the summers. You and me and Mother and Margaret."

"Ah, that's right. When you were little. You caught a crab, and he pinched you, and you screamed like a little girl;

I remember that." Blake laughed; this would be a good trip. "And you were a precocious kid. Used to drive me nuts with all your questions."

He looked around. "Where is my wife? Where's Mary?"

"She's with her sister, Daddy. She's fine. We'll talk to her soon."

"Oh, okay," he said, leaned back in the seat, and closed his eyes. "You and Evelyn still got that thing between you, huh?" Blake glanced at his father, who seemed half asleep.

"That's not my choice. I'm not the one with the problem."

"Your mother used to be a little like that, but I helped her be more forgiving and not so critical of people. You saw her change. I didn't think she'd ever accept you as you are, but she has, all the way. Sure surprised me. Evelyn, now, hates whatever her church tells her to hate. Too bad, because she used to be a nice girl. Pretty, too, like your mother. I told her when she caught you messin' with Jeff that all kids play doctor, and she needed to get over it. I always thought she needed someone to explain the world to her; she wasn't going to learn about it in that fucked up church." He glanced at Blake and said, "Whoops." Blake tried to remember if he'd ever known his father to use the F word. "Where the hell are we? I need to pee." Blake stopped at a convenience store to buy beer and cigars and helped his dad into the men's room.

It was almost dusk when they checked into a motel by the water and sat on the patio drinking beer, smoking cigars, and watching the ripples on the gulf and the fins of dolphins arc slowly toward the setting sun. The lump in Blake's throat grew bigger, and his eyes got wet. He'd had a good childhood, despite being sometimes paralyzed with fear that he'd give himself away. But a lot was forgotten, and a lot of memories of those days had faded from his father's mind, and probably, one day, would disappear from his, too. That fear wouldn't leave him; almost all of James's relatives had ended their lives in the terrible fog of dementia.

The light from the setting sun became a rose glow on the horizon in the darkening sky. Blake loved to look at the stars here; there were so many more than in the city. A meteor fell into the gulf, leaving a long trail of light that faded quickly in the deep blue sky. Blake made a wish that somehow his memories would never die, that he might manage to keep them safe and pass them on to the ones to come. He wished he could see into his father's mind, absorb the record of his life, and feel what it was to be him, and keep his memories alive, too.

It troubled him that all the living we do, all the experiences we have, vanish and cease to exist the moment we close our eyes for the last time. He wanted to understand who his father was apart from the man he knew; the father, the breadwinner, the man who picked him up from school on days when his mother suffered a migraine or took to her bed with cramps. He wanted to see what James's life had been before he'd been burdened with a family, and how he'd learned so much about everything.

James said, "I wish I remembered things better. It's frustrating, like when you wake up after a dream and know you had one but can't recall much of it. Sometimes the bits and pieces don't make sense, but you know they're important."

"I'll tell you about those memories, Dad. I'll keep them safe. Who knows, they might decide to come back to you."

James looked at the sky through tears in his eyes. It was now the deepest black and brimming with stars. Blake touched his hand. "You've had a wonderful life, Dad. Whether you remember all of it's not important. You made a lot of people happy; they'll always remember you."

"I hope so. It's been a good life, even with the bad things. And I wasn't a saint, you know. But, overall, it's been pretty wonderful."

"Nobody's perfect, Dad. But there's more to come. First off, we're gonna find out about Chief, and we're gonna have a blast doing it."

"If we're making memories, I hope they stick around."
"Don't worry, I have a feeling they will."

CHAPTER 3

Mrs. Hoggett

The next day, the two men were feeling the bumps on a dusty dirt road. Near-blinding flashes of sunlight pierced through the live oak branches into the cool shadows of the trees, and Blake asked James, "Are we getting close?"

James said, "It looks that way," and felt he'd been there before; that the smells of cow dung and jasmine blooming somewhere were familiar; then, suddenly, he remembered, like seeing a friend from long ago when his name finally comes to you. This place used to be home; he remembered the farm, even though unsure of how he got there, in that car, at that moment, and hoped the young man driving it was someone he knew. "Turn right at the mailbox," he said, pointing to a spot farther up the road.

The driver turned to him and said, "You sure this is it? Are you excited, Dad?"

"We'll see how I feel when we get there," James answered, relieved that he now recognized the man behind the wheel. It was his son, but he couldn't think of his name. It would come to him; things usually did if he gave it time.

They rode along a two-rut dirt lane through a stand of trees that led into a clearing of grass and dandelions teeming with yellow butterflies. The old house stood at the back end of the field, its single story of peeling white clapboard and faded green shutters protected by a covered porch that ran the entire front of it. It was larger and grander than Blake had imagined. There was gingerbread trim on the porch railings and posts, and flower boxes, now empty, hung beneath the tall windows.

James said, "I remember Momma and Daddy arguing about those flower boxes. Momma said she was going to have them even though Daddy said they were a silly expense when they had so many mouths to feed. Then I came home from school one day and there they were, brand new and painted green. Mama was outside planting marigolds in them. She loved marigolds. She did plant squash in one of them to appease Daddy a little. Momma usually got what she wanted, 'cause she never asked for much."

"How old were you?"

"I was in the third grade, about eight or nine. Momma was pregnant, I remember that. I don't remember with who. She lost a couple of babies, you know."

They climbed the creaking front porch steps, and Blake held James's arm since he looked unsteady. The house was empty; it was left to James and his siblings, but none of them wanted to live there. Even so, they hadn't gotten around to selling it. Blake figured it was because they didn't want to part with the memories. They had agreed to share the expense of keeping it up but didn't want to rent it out to strangers, either. "Somebody needs to plant something in those boxes," James said.

"We don't have the key, Dad. Should we break in?"

"No," James answered. "We'd have to buy a new lock, and that would mean a trip to town and back. We can look in the windows. Not much in there, anyway. Just empty rooms."

Blake tested the windows, hoping to find one that might open. At the back of the house, he found the door to the porch bathroom unlocked and crawled through the little window into the kitchen. He stood for a moment in the big room, then let James in through the front door.

James hesitated at the threshold and said, "Nobody home, is there? I don't want to get shot."

"No, Dad, we're all alone. Want to look around?"

"Not really. I..." He stopped speaking and looked at Blake, his lips quivered and tears dampened his eyes. "Is my momma in here?" Blake could see his father being drawn into the past, and his face appeared to change to a younger version. He walked to the back of the house, into the green linoleum-floored kitchen, jiggled the handle on the water pump at the sink, and stood, silent.

A familiar voice said, "James, I told you not to wash up in there. Go in the bathroom for that. But hurry, lunch is ready."

"Okay, okay, I'm coming." James looked through the kitchen window to the field outside, lush with big-leafed okra plants ready to be picked. "We're not having okra, I hope. I hate okra." He smelled the perfume of stewed collard greens and fried pork chops and walked into the dining room where his family sat waiting at the big oak table. They were smiling at him, and his brother pulled out a chair. "Hurry up, James. We're hungry and thought you'd never get here."

He put his hand on his brother's and sat at the table. "I had a long way to come. But I'm here now."

"Dad, you okay? We need to go now to see your old neighbors, the Hoggetts, and see if they might remember Chief. Are you ready? They're expecting us." James looked up at Blake, then back at the dining table. His family had finished, he supposed; there was no one and nothing there, not even a dish.

"Okay. Let's go. It looks like everybody's left, anyway." As James passed the kitchen, he heard dishes being stacked and saw his mother bending over the sink. She smiled at him, took off her apron, and held her arms out toward him, but as he reached for her, she disappeared.

During the half-hour trip to the Hoggetts' house, James dozed while Blake drove the pristine gray highway lined with neatly mowed grass and wildflowers. More butterflies floated in the warm air. He loved the fresh, untouched look of the country here and considered making it his home someday. A fantasy played in his unusually peaceful mind; he was a boy in dungarees, carrying a BB gun into the woods. A younger boy waited for him. Blake leaned his gun against a tree and hugged him. They kissed on the cheeks and the boy began fondling him, unzipping his jeans, and slipping his hand in to touch him. Blake dropped his pants, and the boy knelt in front of him...

"Can I ask you a question, son?"

Damn, Blake thought, *that was a nice little fantasy to have interrupted.*

"Sure, Dad. What do you want to know?"

"Well, I was just wondering if you ever, you know, if you ever had anything to do with..." James's voice trailed to a whisper.

"Girls?" Blake looked at his dad and frowned. "Only once. Didn't enjoy it."

"Okay. Are we there yet?"

Blake laughed, relieved that the question had been asked and answered at last. "Almost, Dad."

A movement in front of his face got his attention; he swiped the air with his hand and caught a yellow butterfly that had come from the field. Blake slowed the car, lowered his window, and nudged carefully along his palm until it flew out into the sun.

Mrs. Hoggett opened the screen door, and the smells of violet toilet water and fresh-baked cookies wafted from her little over-decorated living room. She kissed Blake's cheek, hugged James with her more than ample arms, and invited the men into the air conditioning. "It's so hot today. I dread the summer!" She pulled Blake to her chest and said, "I can't believe I'm seeing you two. You could have knocked me over with a feather when I got your letter. Have a seat. I've got iced tea ready. Y'all like tea cakes?"

She went into her kitchen, leaving Blake to peruse the room. There were pigs everywhere; paintings of pigs on the walls, piglet printed coasters, a needlepoint pig hassock, an assortment of ceramic hogs on the mantlepiece, and a pair of cloven-foot-shaped slippers in the corner.

Mrs. Hoggett returned with a tray of her best tall crystal glasses, engraved with cartoon piglets and full of sweet tea and sprigs of mint from her garden. She offered a plate of small, round, white-powdered cookies, the aroma of which made Blake's mouth water and brought back memories of his grandmother.

She took a sip of tea, looked at Blake, and said, "You're all grown up! My lord, the last time I laid eyes on you, you were, what, thirteen years old? And James, you're as hand-some as always. How's Mary? Wish she could've come, too."

Blake said, "Mother wanted to visit her sisters in Crossville, and we might be gone for a while. Depends on what we find out."

Mrs. Hoggett sucked in her breath. "Oh, yes, that horse. He was unforgettable. Such a beautiful animal. James wouldn't let me ride him though, because I was a girl, I guess."

"We want to find out how he spent the rest of his life and where he died. It's important to Dad."

She looked at James, sitting deep in an overstuffed armchair, and asked in a loud voice, "Is that right, James? That horse of yours... I can't remember his name."

"Chief," James yelled back, glancing at Blake with a half-smile and a shrug of his shoulders.

"Dad remembers Chief; all about him," Blake said. "But he never found out where they took him after he was sold."

"Well, the man that bought him from your daddy lived a few miles from us, and I remember seeing the trailer go by our house with Chief's blonde tail sticking out the back of it the day they took him off. What a sad thing to see; him going away. James must've been heartbroken that his daddy sold him, but at least he was still close by. Then somebody out of town bought him and I felt so sorry for James because he couldn't spend time with him anymore. I think they took him to Alabama."

She looked at James and said, "So I heard you're having memory problems like the rest of us old-timers." She laughed and blotted the perspiration from her enormous white décolletage with a tiny handkerchief. "Good that you can remember your horse, though." She leaned closer to James and yelled, "Do you remember who I am, James? I'm that girl that lived down the road from you. You took me to the Spring Frolic dance when we were Freshmen, remember? You walked me home and tried to kiss me in the bushes on the way!"

James said, "Yeah, I remember. I wasn't deaf then, either. Just a little near-sighted."

Blake choked on a sip of tea and coughed. "They're afraid he has Alzheimer's. It's progressing gradually, but he knows the situation, and we want to do things while he's still able."

"Well, I asked Hector if he remembers anything about Chief. You know Hector, James? My husband? Well, he gave me the name and address of somebody in Mobile; his daddy used to know him, but he didn't have his phone number. He said he might be able to tell you where Chief went after he bought and sold him. He heard it might have been to a carnival that came through." She started to hand James the paper with the address on it, but gave it to Blake instead. "I hope that helps. That'd be something if you tracked him down. You've got to let me know what you find out, okay?"

"Of course we will. Thank you so much for your help, and tell Hector how much we appreciate it."

"Oh, I will. By the way, Blake, did you ever get married? You being such an attractive child, we always figured you'd have the ladies all over you."

"No, ma'am, I never did. I got too busy with my work; that's just how it goes sometimes."

James moved to stand when Mrs. Hoggett said, "Well, I hoped you might meet my niece while you're here. She's single and a nice lady. Pretty, too. I imagine you'd enjoy making her acquaintance. She's coming for dinner tonight, and y'all are welcome to stay. I'm making a nice pork butt roast."

"Too bad we're only here for a little while. But thanks for the invitation. We're gonna have to run now, though; Dad needs his nap or he gets antsy this time of the afternoon. I guess we'll be going to Mobile early in the morning if I can reach this gentleman. Thanks again for everything, and for that delicious tea and those wonderful cookies."

"Hang on one minute," she said, disappeared into the kitchen and returned with a brown paper bag, handed it to James, and said, "Here's a few more cookies for the road. Lord knows I don't need them!" As she gave the bag to Blake, she thought, *I wonder if he's a little funny.*

Blake pulled James out of the chair that had engulfed him. "Thanks, Ruby-Ann, for helping. You be good and stay out of the bushes." Mrs. Hoggett giggled. "You might be slipping a little yourself in the memory department. You got more than a kiss after that dance."

CHAPTER 4
Southern Hospitality

They spent the night in a motel somewhere between Cedar Grove and Mobile Bay. Blake lay in his bed watching television while his father slept, talking loudly in his sleep and throwing the quilt onto the floor. Blake covered him with the sheet, only to do it again in an hour. He couldn't sleep and went to the balcony and smoked a cigarette; he was determined to give up the habit for good after the trip was over, and maybe quit alcohol, too. The cigarette made him crave a bourbon and water.

He thought of his dad's comment about Evelyn catching him and his cousin hiding behind a hibiscus bush in the gazebo when she went to water her palms. James called it "playing doctor", even though he was well aware of what they'd been up to. They were too old to call it play, and his aunt knew it. She screamed at them, "Y'all are going to hell!" as the boys fumbled desperately to pull up their jeans.

She didn't want any perverts in her house and threatened to tell his dad, and did. Blake heard her inside the house saying in her loudest whisper, "Those boys are out there being queers!"

His father said, "Leave them alone. I'll talk to them. Don't you say another word about it." She ran straight to Blake's mother to fill her in, gloating that both of her sisters had spawned sick and twisted children, and it made her glad that she'd never had any. Apparently, the disease ran in the family. Blake's mother took to her bedroom, got under the covers, and cried all afternoon. She refused to come out, even for supper.

The next morning, not a word concerning the incident was uttered by anyone, as if it had never happened. But, as she passed Blake the bacon, his aunt glared at him and pursed her lips upward as if he had passed gas.

Blake got back in bed and fell asleep, despite his dad's snoring. He awoke early, had coffee and tea cakes, and then phoned Mobile Information to get the number he needed. He sweet-talked a couple of operators, then a supervisor who said she'd call the number, and the people could call him back if they wanted to. "Please tell them I'm trying to find the where-abouts of a horse named Chief".

Less than an hour later, the phone rang. A man's voice said, "Hello, this is Jordan Johnson. I'm George Johnson's son, the man who bought Chief from somebody in Florida. If you're heading over this way, I'd be glad to meet and tell you what I remember."

"Over this way" was 200 miles to Mobile, and by after-noon, they crossed the state line and the bay, then stopped just inside the Mobile city limits to look at the map and get their bearings. James had to pee, so they stopped at a gas station, filled the tank, and Blake got directions from the attendant, who said, "You'd better change your clothes before you go into that neighborhood." A few miles later, they drove a red brick street with an oak- canopied park on the left, thick with Spanish moss, and Gone-With-the-Wind houses on the right; antebellum mansions like the ones that had survived in a few southern cities.

They stopped in front of the house, and a man on the big white Corinthian-columned front porch stood up from his rocking chair and waved. He came toward them on the walk and yelled, "You Blake? Come on up the driveway."

Blake parked the car, and the man came to greet them and shook Blake's hand. "My name's Cooper; Jordan will be right down." He shook James's hand, too, and directed them through the big front doors. Blake glanced at James and could see he was confused, but not panicked.

Inside stood an enormous curved staircase, and a voice from the top said, "I'm coming!" Two huge furry feet with enormous, long red toenails descended the steps.

Blake whispered, "What the fuck?" and looked at his dad.

The owner of the feet came into view and said, "I'm Jordan Johnson. Nice to meet y'all. Don't mind the shoes. Cooper dares me to wear them when we're having visitors. Everybody swears this house is haunted, and he likes to give them a scare."

Blake complimented the man's home: high ceilings hung with antique crystal chandeliers; huge oil portraits in gilt frames, velvet and marble everywhere. He smelled the musty odor of years that had passed; the dust of a nearly forgotten time, and heard the rustle of crinoline sweeping through the room.

Jordan said, "Thanks. It's not my style, but when you inherit something, you try not to look a gift horse in the mouth. I have to admit, though, I love living here. I guess it's in my blood, and this is all we're left with." He motioned Blake and James through an archway and into the parlor.

Cooper wheeled a cocktail cart into the room and said, "After your drive, you must be ready for some relaxation. Who needs a drink?"

Blake smiled and said, "Is that bourbon I see? I'd love one with a splash. Thank you. Dad, you want a snort?"

James looked at Cooper and said, "I'd love a whiskey, neat. Whatever kind you've got. I wouldn't know one from the other anymore. My wife doesn't let me keep any in the house."

"Well, we won't tell her, I promise," Jordan said, laughing.

James stared hard at him and asked Blake, "Who is this guy? Do we know him? He knows my wife?"

"It's okay, Dad. This man's going to help us find Chief. He's a friend. Sorry, Jordan; Dad gets a little mixed up."

Jordan said, "I understand what y'all are going through. It runs in my family. It doesn't bother me. You're a good son."

They drank into the afternoon and snacked on tiny sandwiches that Cooper made. They moved onto the big screened-in side porch to enjoy the breeze off the Gulf. James dozed in a wicker rocking chair while Jordan talked about Chief. Cooper was quick to add what he could to the conversation and appeared to have been a part of Jordan's life for a long time. He smiled at Jordan as he told his story, and Jordan returned the smile, and the tone of the conversation changed, aided by the whiskey, from politeness to easy intimacy.

"I remember my father talking about a beautiful palomino he'd bought from a man in Florida, in a little town near Tallahassee, but I don't have a clue what the name was. Dad was friends with the Governor, and he told Daddy about Chief; how beautiful he was, and that he was for sale." Jordan said. "I've looked through my dad's papers but have found nothing concerning Chief; I'm gonna keep at it. He left a lot of things I still need to sort through. Something might turn up."

Blake said, "Well, he was first sold in Cedar Grove, but we don't know where they took Chief after that, but that's where your father bought him. Doesn't matter, though. The thing we care about is where he ended up."

"Well, I wish I knew that," Jordan answered, "but Dad had a rancher friend in Texas who bought horses from him before I came along. That would've been before my dad bought Chief. It makes sense that's where he sent your horse. I was too young to remember that, but Dad took me to that ranch when I was a boy, to visit his friend and have a little break from my mother. Dad didn't drink around his wife, either."

He smiled and looked at James, now awake and

listening to the conversation.

James perked up and said, "Women like to make it their job to keep us out of trouble. One of their jobs, anyway. It worked for me, dammit."

Jordan laughed and asked Cooper, "Can you do me a favor and go up to Dad's office and bring down that cedarwood box by the file cabinet? It's full of old pictures and postcards. There might be something about that ranch in it."

Jordan poured them all another drink, toasted Chief, and wished them luck in finding him. Cooper returned with several pieces of paper in his hand, gave them to Jordan, and said, "This might save you a lot of time looking."

Jordan took them and said, "You are a dear, thanks." Handing the papers to Blake, he said, "Mystery solved. Cooper keeps tabs on everything in this house."

Blake held up one piece so that his father could see it: a postcard with a photo of a corral under a blue sky and a pretty girl on a horse in front of it. The girl wore a cowboy hat, a tiny short skirt, and snakeskin thigh boots. The caption read "Come Take a Ride at Annabelle Ranch!" And under that, "We Got a Filly For You! The Most Fun In Fort Worth!"

Blake said, "It would seem..."

Jordan laughed and said, "All I remember of that trip is the heat and the horses, and the pretty girls that played games with me while Dad went out hunting. He'd be gone a long time, and always came back in a good mood."

Blake looked at James and said, "Well, Dad, it's a long way, but I guess we'd better head for Texas."

James said, "Why Texas? I hate Texas."

"We might find out about Chief there," Blake answered.

"I've told you, Chief is dead. A long time ago. I was a boy."

"Yes, Dad. I'll explain later."

Blake looked at another piece of paper. It was a letterhead with a note written in a manly longhand: "Thanks for letting me buy the horse. She's a damned beauty and you know how we both love blondes! Come back soon!" It was signed *A M*. Blake looked at Cooper and said, "Damn! This is it for sure, I bet!"

Jordan said, "Where was it from?"

Blake shook his head. "Looks like the sender's address was torn off. But it's got to be from your father's friend."

"Wish I knew who A M was," Cooper said.

"You guys will find out. I can't wait to know myself," Jordan said. He reached for Blake and squeezed his shoulder. "How about some dinner?"

Blake said, "Thanks, but I think those sandwiches were plenty."

Cooper said, "Well, you'd better stay the night. You can start in the morning. I'll make you breakfast. It's six hundred miles to Fort Worth."

Cooper showed the men to their enormous room, filled with antiques and two double beds, with a view of the park and the bay beyond it. "If you prefer," he said, "I can put you in separate rooms. I figured you'd want to be with your dad in case he needs something."

"Yes, this is good, thanks."

Cooper leaned close to Blake and whispered, "You ever had a threesome? Jordan wants to know." He grinned and rubbed Blake's shoulder.

"No, sir, never have."

He grinned and said, "Life is short. Maybe you need to get out more." He smiled and waited in vain for Blake to speak.

"Well, if you get lonely, we're in the next room."

"I see. I'll sure keep that in mind." Blake smiled at Cooper and said, "We've got an early day tomorrow. Better get some sleep."

Blake and his father took turns in the bathroom, then climbed into the high antique beds. James closed his eyes and said softly, "You think those guys are..."

"Yes, Dad, I do."

"Well, seems to suit them all right. Goodnight, son."

They left early, after breakfast. Jordan and Cooper stood on the porch waving goodbye like good Southerners, and Jordan yelled, "Take a right when you get to Lafayette!"

They drove west on the Interstate and James napped, waking occasionally to ask, "Where the hell are you taking me? Are we at Chattahoochee yet?" Or, "Pull over, I've got to pee." Blake left the highway, found a gas station, and helped his dad into the men's room. "You gonna hold my pecker for me, too?" his dad laughed. Blake bought a map while he waited and decided they'd stop in Alexandria for the night; it looked to be halfway to Fort Worth. They drove on, and James watched the landscape go by, and began talking.

"I came through these parts once when I was young. I got drafted into the Army and they sent us out here for training. A little place called—I can't remember, but we'd go into town sometimes and have fun. Maybe Brag something-or-other. We'd get a few drinks in us and go dancing. There were always lots of pretty girls hanging around, and they liked meeting us boys. It was the uniforms, I think. Of course, I was good-looking back then. I didn't have any trouble getting dates, if you know what I mean."

"I bet you were, Dad. You're still good-looking."

"Well, there was this girl I met. I fell for her. She was only nineteen, but I wanted to ask her to marry me, then I got sent to California and I never saw her again. We wrote letters, and then she wrote to me she was getting married to a guy she met in Baton Rouge. Never knew what happened to her after that."

"You remember her name?"

"Yes, I remember." James looked out the side window. His voice became a near whisper. "It was Margaret, Margaret Bagley. I still have her letters up in the attic.

"I never told your mother about her, but I wanted to

name your sister after her. Your mother didn't like that name, but I talked her into it. She still has no inkling why I insisted."

Blake chuckled. His dad turned to him and said, "And don't you ever tell her. That's between us. I never told anybody else that secret."

"Don't worry."

"I kind of wish we hadn't named her that now. If I'd known your sister would turn out to be such a—". He stopped himself from saying it.

"Bitch?"

"Yep. That's the word. And my Margaret could never be like that." James shook his head and looked at his hands, now clasped together in his lap.

They stayed silent for twenty miles. Blake had a memory rising in his mind, one that he'd always treasured but had never spoken of to his dad, and he wanted to change the subject.

"Dad," he said, "Do you remember once when you took me hunting, and we ended up hiking off the road into a pine plantation, and you taught me how to call the vultures?"

"Remind me, son."

"We carried our shotguns and walked into the middle of an acre of pine trees, and you told me to lie on the pine needles and be absolutely still. We lay there in that beautiful forest of longleaf pines that smelled like heaven and were planted in rows far enough apart so you could see the sky. It felt like a church in there. I didn't understand at first what we were doing. You said, 'Stay quiet and don't move.' It seemed like a long time; I fell asleep for a while, but woke up when you hissed and said, 'Wake up but don't move a muscle.' I opened my eyes, and the sky was full of vultures circling above us, getting lower and lower and closer and closer, and soon I could see their heads, and their eyes looking at us, and I realized what you had done: called the damned vultures. I was sure you were magic, like an Indian shaman."

"You mean like buzzards? I was told by my grandma

that I had a gift for those things; maybe calling vultures is one of them. She said I got it from her. Back then, she was kind of famous for doing spells and curing what ailed people, and knowing secret things about the woods and the weather. The Indians taught her that stuff when she was little. My dad taught me about surviving in the woods, and how to call the animals. I wanted you to learn those things, too. Did the birds light?"

"Yes, Dad, they did. Scared the shit out of me. I thought for sure they'd eat us."

James laughed, "Did they?"

"No," Blake said. "We kept laying there, and they came out of the trees and sat in a ring around us on the ground and stared. I could smell their stink. It was spooky as hell. I guess they were trying to decide if we were dead or not. Then you sat up and said 'Boo!' and they couldn't fly out of there fast enough. Their wings were so big I didn't see how they could get through the trees without hitting them. It was sort of funny and felt like a dream. I figured we fooled death that day. That's one of my favorite childhood memories, and of you."

"I don't remember."

James's words hit Blake in the pit of his stomach. Maybe, Blake thought, we need to have lunch soon.

CHAPTER 5

Wildflower Dreams

They traveled on, through the bowels of the South, and stopped at Baton Rouge for lunch, then reached Lafayette and turned right as Cooper had instructed them. James slept, woke, and slept again, sometimes waking to ask their whereabouts and where his wife was, and wondering to himself how he got in this car with this man he sort of felt like he might know. The man spoke to him, so he nodded and said, "I'm fine; don't worry about me. Are we getting close?" or, "I might have to pee real soon".

Blake left the interstate and drove into a tiny town that seemed devoid of people. They passed three cemeteries and several churches, all Baptist of different flavors, and he thought, *God, what a life. Spend it in church and then die. I would've been lynched for looking too long at the pastor's son. Or maybe I'd marry some teenage girl, the prettiest in town, whose father owned a big pig farm, and then have lots of kids, or at least as many times as I could manage with her. And my whole life spent trying to hide that I wanted that gorgeous preacher's son.*

He enjoyed creating this imaginary life; time passed quicker that way. *One day, my F-150 would have a flat tire and I'd see the man I wanted out in the field on his big stallion, and he'd come over and change the tire for me, saying I might get my clothes dirty, even though I had on my overalls. I'd help him put the flat in the back, and our hands would touch, our eyes would meet, and I would realize my youth had been wasted in this awful place. We'd walk into the field and make love in the yellow wildflowers, their perfume would overtake our senses, and he'd tell me he'd been watching me all these years. We'd lie there afterward and feel the butterflies landing on our sun-warmed, bare skin.*

"Son, I wasn't kidding about having to pee! Can you stop daydreaming and pull over now?" James was awake and seemed to recognize his son. Blake parked the car on the shoulder and helped James out, and the two of them stood side by side and relieved themselves into the wildflowers behind an oak tree.

"Well, that's one time we got to do this," Blake said. "We'll have to find some cigars tonight." He smiled; his thoughts still wallowed in yellow and butterflies.

James said, "Don't worry, there's a town up the road. They're bound to have a smoke shop. I remember now. It's not Brag, it's Braggville, and I want to stop there."

Miles later, the men entered the tired-looking town. James stared out the window in silence, trying to remember something, shaking his head. "No, I still can't figure it out," he said, as if repeating the word might help him remember where he was, or as if there was a Rolodex in his mind, spinning to find the right index card. "It sure has changed from what I remember. Go down towards the river and look for a little cafe named after a flower, I think, or a lady's name. It's down on the riverfront. Bars and such down there. Us soldiers used to hang out there a lot and have a good time." He closed his eyes and then said, "Was it Irish? No, something like that, dammit, I can't remember."

"Like an iris flower, Dad?" Blake said.

"Yes! That's it, the Iris! The Wild Iris Cafe. I sure would like to find that place."

"Turn here," James said, pointing the way. They drove down a street that led toward the riverfront. James stared ahead, searching the storefronts on the empty street. "Stop! That's it, son; that's the Iris." The street was almost empty, with only several cars parked on it, and just a few of the buildings with lights on.

As he parked the car, Blake said, "Doesn't look like much to me. There's no sign, either. It must be closed up."

"I'm sure that's the Iris. That was a long time ago. The food wasn't very good, but they had cheap beer, and we always had fun. Must have closed after the soldiers left. Let's look in the window."

They crossed the street and stood in front of the red brick building. The sun was going down. James peered into the gloom of the big room, empty except for a few tables and chairs and a bar along the wall. The faded image of a purple flower remained visible on the plate glass. The lettering was almost gone, peeling and cracked; it had fluttered to the floor long ago like snowflakes and left an outline in glue: The Wild Iris Cafe.

A voice from behind them broke the silence. It came from a man standing on the sidewalk who looked at them with suspicion and asked, "You guys looking for something? They're not open; I guess you can tell." The slightest hint of a sneer touched his lips.

Blake nodded. "We hoped they might still be in business. My father here used to hang out with his buddies from the training base back in the day. We're passing through and he wanted to see it again."

"It's been closed up for years." The man put his hands in his pockets and looked at James, his expression softening. "I mighta been there the same times you were. It was the place to go back then, that's for sure. Seems like every pretty girl in Braggville used to go there, not that this burgh was crawling with them, but we had our share of good-looking women."

James said, "You know, you seem kind of familiar to me. That laugh... Did we know each other? My mind isn't what it used to be; I wish I could remember things better."

"My name's Duncan DuBois. Yeah, you're familiar to me, too. Small world, eh?"

Blake said, "I'll bet you two could dredge up some

memories if you tried." He turned and looked through the big window into the darkening cafe while the two old soldiers compared recollections of the Wild Iris. Blake could imagine it softly lit with incandescent lights, and full of young people, some in uniform, girls in their prettiest dresses, all of them laughing, arms draped around shoulders, beer bottles hoisted toward the tin-tiled ceiling, shining and new through the cigarette smoke.

Blake imagined being there, standing at the far end of the bar, laughing with a friend, and taking a drink from his bottle of beer. A young man came through the front doors and looked in his direction. It was the preacher's son from the town down the highway, the man from the field of flowers. He smiled at Blake. *Damn, he's handsome,* Blake thought.

The man stopped at the other end of the bar, his gaudy, flowered aloha shirt glowing in the dim room. A few of the friends slapped him on the back, some hugged him, and a pretty girl shoved a beer bottle into his palm. He drank and looked at Blake. The crowd parted, opening a path for him to walk to where Blake stood, smiling. They embraced, and Blake heard applause and people yelling, "Kiss him! For god's sake, kiss him!" so he did; a long, warm, happy kiss, and the applause grew louder, and the room filled with the sound of people singing "Let Me Call You Sweetheart". More kisses, and the man whispered into Blake's ear, "Don't worry, you'll be back. We'll build a redwood cabin somewhere in the mountains and always be this way; happy."

Someone from behind placed a hand on his shoulder, and he turned to see his father looking curiously at him. "Where the hell were you, son? I was afraid you'd gone deaf."

"No, I was imagining how much fun you must have had here. I'm glad you did."

"Well, things are about to get better. My old friend here says he knows where Margaret is, and it's not the cemetery. He'll take us to see her tomorrow if we want to go. I said hell yes, even though the sight of me might scare her to death."

Blake was skeptical and thought that the stranger could be wrong and was getting his father's hopes up for nothing. But if it was true, he was glad; his father would be happy to see his old love again.

They got a room at the Holiday Inn. They left Duncan standing on the street in front of the cafe; he'd given them directions to the hotel out on the highway, and they'd made plans to meet the next day. Blake started the car, and as they pulled away, his father looked back and started singing to himself:

> "Let me call you sweetheart,
> I'm in love with you,
> Let me hear you whisper,
> That you love me too..."

Blake slowed the car and looked at James. "Dad, why are you singing that song?"

"No clue. It popped into my head. Must be some memory trying to get through. I always liked that song." He turned to the window and started humming the tune again.

As they lay in their hotel beds, James seemed to be dead to the world, but Blake lay awake on the crisp sheets and relived his fantasy. He wondered about the lover he'd invented, who seemed so real and loving and the kind of man he'd always wanted to find. He slept and dreamed of fields of flowers and music from before his time.

Duncan arrived at the hotel, and Blake offered to buy breakfast in the 60s-decorated hotel restaurant, a style that set Blake's teeth on edge; Duncan talked about Margaret to prepare James for his meeting with her.

"Margaret started to fail a few years ago, her mind, anyway. She's still a beautiful woman for her age, and sweet as can be, like always. For a time, she had mostly good days, but I'm afraid they don't happen as often now. Sometimes it seems that she remembers me, but I'm never sure if she's just trying to be nice and not let on she has no clue who I am. She was like that, remember? She wanted everyone to feel important."

Blake could see that James was upset; he had tears clinging to the rims of his eyes as he looked at Duncan and listened to him speak words that hurt him. His disappointment was obvious and heartbreaking; he'd had hopes of something far more romantic.

"Will she remember me?" James asked.

"Probably not. I doubt it. Some days she can't even talk but stares at you like she's not there anymore, you know what I mean?"

"That might kill me to see her like that. At least she's alive," James said. "But I'm not sure that's a good thing."

Blake said, "So, Duncan, how did you meet Margaret?"

"Well," he said, taking a sip of coffee, "When she worked in a bank in Baton Rouge during the summer break to save some money for college. She was staying with relatives down there. I don't remember their names. I walked into the bank one day to cash my government check, and she helped me. She looked so damned pretty, and so sweet; I knew I was in trouble.

"I asked her out, and we had a nice time at the movies and dinner. A few days later, I got sent up here for training. We kept in touch for months, and one day she came back to Braggville to live. She got a job waitressing at the Iris to tide her over until she could go to college. She wanted to be an artist. Everybody said she'd be crazy to waste her time on that, but it turned out she had a lot of talent. She ended up making a living selling her paintings, mostly in New Orleans, but some as far away as New York. I was real proud of her for that."

Blake said, "So you saw her again up here?"

"Yeah, we started dating again and damned if I didn't get orders to go to England. Things were getting awfully bad over there. I wanted to marry her and to make sure I came back in one piece. She deserved that."

"You went to war in England?" James asked, a memory

forming in his mind. His eyes got wide. "Goddammit, I remember you now, and when you dated Margaret. That's all I remember, except my jealousy."

"Shit, I thought it was you, just couldn't believe it," Duncan said. "It's a long time to hold a grudge, but all these years I've been mad at you. I go off to war, and you steal my girl. Of course, nobody could stay mad at you long because we all loved you so much. We practically lived in that bar, and most of the time it seemed pretty boring until you'd walk in and, just like that, it was a party!"

James said, "I had to leave her, too. I felt so bad about having to go away, 'cause I fell in love with Margaret and she fell in love with me. Anyway, you left without asking her to wait. She told me that."

"All right, I'll give you that much. When I got back and she told me what had happened, I felt like I'd die of either heartache or hate. But she loved you so much, I let her go so she'd be happy like that for life."

"Dad, where'd you meet Margaret?"

"At the Iris when she worked there. I asked her out, but she turned me down; said she had no time to date in those days." Looking at Duncan, he said, "I think she was still trying to be faithful to her beau in England."

"Well, that's something at least," Duncan said.

James said, "One day, I was driving back to camp, and her little car was on the side of the road with a flat tire. I stopped to help, changed the tire for her, and, well, we kind of got carried away. She told me she'd decided not to wait anymore, and she'd wanted to be with me since the time we met. We took a walk in the field. That time of the year, the wildflowers bloom, and it was so romantic we kind of lost control. I can't believe I'd almost forgotten that day. Memories come and go. But when we kissed goodbye that day out in the field, the blue ribbon in her hair fell to the grass. I tied her hair up for her with it; she didn't want to be mussed up when she got back home. She giggled and said, 'That's my favorite ribbon,' and I said, 'It matches your eyes.'

"We became a couple, and it didn't take long for us to talk about getting married. But I got orders to go out to California, and we didn't know how long it would be.

"I asked her to wait, and I'd try my best to get her out there to be with me. We both thought we might like California and had a dream about a cabin up in the redwoods. It would've been so nice.

"Everyone heard I got my orders. They got together and had a going-away party for me at the Iris. All the soldiers were in uniform. I kept looking for Margaret, but couldn't find her anywhere. Someone said she had the night off, but soon she came through the doors looking like a princess in a dress with yellow flowers on it. She pushed her way through the crowd, and they started yelling, 'Kiss her, kiss her!' So I did, and they sang that song, "Let Me Call You Sweetheart." James looked surprised and said to Blake, "That's why I sang that yesterday! It was a memory I'd forgotten about!"

A few moments passed in silence until Blake asked Duncan why he was at the Iris the day before. He answered, "I had to go there to meet a man interested in buying the Iris building, but he didn't show. On the way to my car, I saw you two and wondered who you were. No reason to be there nowadays unless you're doing something shady. I own the building that the Iris occupied — I bought it soon after it closed — I didn't want anything bad to happen to it."

"Well, you being there is pretty strange, don't you think? Seems like quite a coincidence," Blake said, looking at Duncan through narrowed eyes.

"Stranger things happen in Louisiana all the time. We don't think twice about them."

"So," Duncan said, half-smiling at James, "What happened when you went to California?"

"Not much, if I remember, and there's lots I don't now; only a few years of Army bullshit. I decided I didn't like it out west, and when I got discharged, I took my time and drove home across the country. I got here and went straight to the Iris. You see, Margaret had written to me that she got engaged to some guy she met in Baton Rouge. She stopped answering my letters. I figured she got hurt when I stayed so long out west without asking her to join me. I don't remember why I didn't, to tell the truth. Time got away from me, and she got tired of waiting. She wanted a family, and it looked like she'd have to make a move soon or she'd never have one."

"I got to the Iris, and of course, she didn't still work there. The bartender told me she'd got married and moved to New Orleans and was getting famous because of her paintings, and her husband owned the biggest car dealership in Louisiana. So, she was all set.

"I got back in my roadster and drove to Florida. I didn't care where I ended up.

"I stopped in a little town in the panhandle to find some lunch and saw Blake's mother in a dime store selling candy. You can figure out the rest. She's been a good wife and mother, and I love her so much; she gave me a good son and a half-ass daughter, and now I can't remember what I did yesterday, or five minutes ago sometimes, or even where I am."

The waitress brought the check. Duncan asked, "Well, y'all ready to go to the rest home now?"

"How does she look?" James said.

"You might not recognize her, but I'll point her out. I'm the only one that ever goes to check on her. It hurts me that she's like that. It's so hard to see. Sometimes she only stares at me and cries. She's got a couple of kids in New Orleans, but her husband died a few years back. The kids sent her up here to be with her relatives, but they don't seem to give a shit about her, either. They put her in the home. They found out they're not in the will, and she'll die a rich lady. So, I doubt she'll know who you are, James."

"Has she ever asked about me?" James said.

"No, not to me, anyway. Sorry, James, that's the way she is now. Sometimes it seems like she doesn't remember anything at all."

"Let's find out," James said.

The nursing home was a dreary place; Blake could feel the resignation and dejection of the patients. The room tried to look cheerful, despite the ambience of death. Stick-on wall decorations of butterflies and flowers belied the awful truth of it, and the odor of old age, rubbing alcohol and urine destroyed their whimsy. The Lucy Show played on a television in the corner.

James approached Margaret, who looked up at him, her head trembling from side to side. He took her hand, and she seemed to try to speak, but there was no recognition in her eyes, no smile or change of her blank expression. She stared at James for a few moments, then looked at Blake. She lifted her arm toward him and opened her palm as if gesturing for him to come near. Blake stepped forward, took her hand, and she pulled him down to her face, until her lips were at his ear, and whispered, "I remember the flowers."

She dropped his hand and smiled. Blake was confused until he realized she had mistaken him for the James of her youth.

James said, "Margaret, it's me, James. I came a long way to see you." But Margaret's face remained expressionless; her eyes showed nothing; no emotion, no recognition, and no light.

James's eyes grew red and wet, and his bottom lip was quivering as he looked at Blake and Duncan. "Well, that's that, then. If we're going to find my horse, we'd better get going while I can still remember him."

Blake thanked Duncan for his help and said, "Looks like my dad is ready to let go of this one."

James wiped his eyes with his sleeve. "Give her a kiss from me now and then, would you, Duncan? You don't have to say who it's from."

As Blake turned to leave, he saw an insect fly from Margaret's hair and flutter toward the open window. A nurse saw Blake following the tiny butterfly's flight, looked at him, and winked as if they'd shared a secret.

The next morning, Blake woke his father early, and soon they drove away from the past, up the interstate toward Alexandria. James watched the road disappear under the car and imagined the blacktop was vanishing behind him, never to be traveled again.

CHAPTER 6
Madame Psyche

On through Alexandria and to the Texas border; Blake announced it as they crossed. James said, "I hate this place. Drove through it when I came back from California and was afraid I'd die before I got out. That's all I remember, except knowing I'd never want to be there again. It was ugly and dusty and mean and hot as hell. You even had to join the club to buy a drink there. Met a couple of girls, and they were the most forward things I'd ever seen. I never liked women who acted that way."

They drove on, and the landscape turned from pine woods to oil wells on the horizon. They stopped for lunch outside a faded little town, at a cafe surrounded by pickup trucks and jacked-up Jeeps. Inside, it was cool, and a buxom, rouged, middle-aged, cowboy-hat-wearing woman guided them to a table. "Or would you rather have a booth? I got one open over there," she said. Blake nodded yes, and she seated them by the window overlooking the parking lot where men in tight blue denim leaned against their trucks, smoking un-filtered Camels and drinking Lone Star beer from brown bot-tles. Further out from where they stood, empty beer cans were lined up on a wooden fence, and the cowboys were shooting them with their long-barrelled pistols.

Several of the men looked like pinups in a beefcake calendar. Blake thought, *Texas can't be all bad.*

His dad, trying to read the menu, looked up and said,

"You'd better be careful, son. They might string you up for just thinking that."

Blake could feel himself blushing. "I don't know what you mean." He looked back at his menu. "And stop reading my damned mind." James gave him a sly grin. The whole family had learned to watch what they thought around him.

After lunch, James went to the men's room while Blake called his mother from the phone booth out front. She heard the gunshots and asked, "Where in hell are you?"

"Texas," Blake answered.

"Oh, right."

Mary was fine, except her sister was being a bitch, but she was used to that. "Give your dad a kiss from me. Y'all call me when you get to a motel; I'll say hi to him then." He hung up and dialed Information for the number of a hotel in Dallas that Cooper had recommended. It was in the gay entertainment district downtown. He booked a room.

The traffic was light, the weather was clear, and the air conditioner worked hard to protect them from the blast furnace outside. James napped while Blake listened to Top 40 music on the radio. He couldn't find an oldies station and settled for the popular songs that had become empty of romance since his father's time.

James woke up. "Just where are we going, mister? Who are you, anyway?" His voice became vicious. Blake tried not to panic when James got hostile. He wished he knew a way to calm him.

"It's okay, Dad. I'm your son, and we're going to Fort Worth, Texas, to see a man about a horse."

"A horse? You're a lying son of a bitch. You're going to take me off somewhere and leave me. Where is my wife?"

"She's fine and at her sister's house."

"Good lord, the mean one? Poor Mother." He calmed down. "You do look like my son, that's for sure. Anybody ever tell you that? He's better looking, though. He looks like me. I've been sitting here wondering whatever happened to an old girlfriend of mine. We were gonna get married. Her name was Margaret. Seems like it was only yesterday. She was so pretty and sweet."

"Well, maybe we'll look her up sometime."

"That would be nice, but I'm gonna have to pee soon."

The hotel was beautiful; the interior appealed to Blake and made him wish he'd followed up on his long-ago plans to earn a design degree. Its rates were outrageous, but Blake didn't care; he wanted to be pampered after their days of driving. They ate an overpriced Tex-Mex dinner at a table overlooking a street that soon became crowded with young men in a party mood, most of them either handsome or pretty. Several female impersonators strolled the sidewalk, laughing and hugging boys as they passed them. James said, "Those hookers out there... they're kind of tall, don't you think?"

"This is Texas, Dad, and everything's bigger."

"So is that surprise between their legs, I bet." Blake laughed and choked on his bourbon. There was so much left to learn about his father.

"Have you ever seen a drag show, Dad?"

"Yes, as a matter of fact, I have. I've been around, you know. When I was stationed in California, a bunch of us drove up to San Francisco for the weekend and caught a show there, in a bar called Uncle Sam's. Funny, huh? Soldiers in there... It was hard to believe they weren't real women. Most of them were beautiful and talented; they sang and danced like pros. I never told anyone back home that I'd gone there because they might think I was queer. I enjoyed it and was mad as hell when I heard one of them got the crap beat out of her going home that night; it was in the newspaper. She died from her head injuries. I was so mad. She wasn't doing anything wrong."

"It can be dangerous being gay."

"Yes, it can. When I was younger, there were some guys at my school who liked to beat up queers and take their money. Roll 'em, they called it. Sons of bitches. Course, you didn't dare say anything because they'd start looking at you funny if you took the side of the poor guys they beat up. When you came along and got old enough for me to know you were that way, I felt guilty for years that I didn't try to stop those assholes. I thought I was better than that. I'd stop them now. That's because of you. You're a wonderful man, and I'm proud you're my son. Anybody tries to hurt you, I'd kill them and not give a damn."

"Thanks, Dad. I hope you'll never have to, but thanks for the support."

"And, son, I know you're not a kid anymore, but please promise me you'll never do anything you'll regret, something that's not true to who you are. People can do things that haunt them for the rest of their lives."

"I promise." It was the first time he could remember his dad giving him advice more profound than the Boy Scout creed, and to hear the love coming through his father's words made him want to hug him.

So he did, and James patted his back the way he used to when Blake was small and had suffered a horrible injury, perhaps a skinned knee or a bee sting.

Blake leaned back in his chair, had a sip of bourbon, and tried to compose himself. "Dad, if you're up to it, we can go to the show after dinner. They have one in this hotel. But only if you'll be okay. If you get tired, all we have to do is go upstairs."

"Wonder how often a father gets to go to a drag show with his son? It'll be our secret, right?"

"Forever."

The entertainment was racier than Blake had expected; it had been years since he'd been in a gay bar or seen a drag performance. But this was the gayest spot in Texas, and the performers did their best to shock and entertain, and James loved it all.

One performer, Madam Psyche, had a mind-reading act. She told secrets about people in the audience and made jokes about them, and, judging by their embarrassed reactions, her stories were all true. She left the stage, sat on James's lap, kissed him on the cheek, and told the audience, "I bet this handsome fellow has some stories to tell."

James loved the attention and the sultry smell of her perfume. He returned her kiss, then said to Blake, "I'm tired. I want to go to bed now."

Blake fell asleep right away. He dreamed he was in the field of flowers with the young man in his fantasy, then the dream became a nightmare. The flowers turned to brown grass, and their scent changed to the odor of cow dung. His lover yelled, "Get him!" and Blake was running toward someone trying to escape from him. He looked back, and his friend was running for him, too, and was holding a baseball bat in the air. He caught up with him and began beating him. Blake grabbed the man and pulled him down, and searched his pants for a wallet. His lover kept hitting the man. "Don't give him a blowjob, get his money!" Blake looked at him; his handsome face was his own; he had become the one wielding the club.

Blake screamed at himself, "That's enough! Don't kill him!" He found the man's wallet on the ground, picked it up, and ran crying toward the dark forest at the end of the field.

He woke up, shaken. The dream seemed real and significant, but he didn't know what it meant. He looked at the window and the gray night sky. A moth fluttered up from his blanket, flew to the window, and crawled in circles on the glass. Blake went naked and chilly to the window and opened it to the night air and sounds of people on the street below. The moth landed on his hand for a moment, as if to say thank you, then flew into the smoke-scented darkness toward the distant street lamp.

Morning came, and the sunlight was blinding; Blake hadn't closed the drapes after he'd released the moth. He looked down at the street and saw a van parked there and a group of men standing beside it. A uniformed man was unloading suitcases and boxes from the back of the vehicle.

One man stomped his feet, screamed something, and rushed into the hotel lobby.

James was awake and in the bathroom. The shower was running, and Blake yelled, "Dad, do you want breakfast? Are you hungry?"

They sat in a booth in the hotel restaurant. A young man stood at the table next to them, looked their way, and said, "Oh, hey! You're those handsome hunks at the show!"

Blake recognized him as the drag queen who had sat on his father's lap; the remnants of last night's eyeliner now only a shadow. James said, "Who the hell is that?"

"I'm Madame Psyche from the drag show, honey, don't you remember? I was a lot prettier last night. But everybody loved *you*. Were you trying to steal my act?"

James looked mystified and stared at the man, squinting his eyes as if trying to remember. Blake said, "He's my father, and he has memory problems. Last night might come back to him later. But you were great. We both enjoyed the show."

"Thanks, hon!" Madame Psyche said. "Listen, would it be all right if I slid in with you? I hate being alone at a four-top. And there's some people here I don't want joining me."

Blake moved over to let him in.

"My real name's Seth."

Blake introduced himself and James, and Seth began telling his story. He was part of a drag group on their way to Los Angeles, with a booking in Phoenix, too. "Everything's been going fine until the van broke down this morning. The driver's trying to find a mechanic, but he wants us to give him money up front to fix it, and most of our party pissed off to the airport without me because I can't afford the expense; we live on tips until we get paid next month, so that leaves just me and Lady Pernod to get to Phoenix. We've got a show there next week. How can I get there with all my shit?"

James smiled and looked at Blake. "Who the hell is this?"

"He was in the show last night. I guess you forgot."

"No, I remember some pretty women dancing around, but not this guy."

Seth laughed. "So, I guess I fooled you. Thank god I've still got some talent."

A man approached the table and in a deep voice said to Seth, "Honey, I bought a Greyhound ticket back to St. Louis. I'm quitting this shit show. Good luck. Keep in touch and let me know when you're back home."

He looked at Blake and James and said, "I'm Miss Pernod. You might have seen me last night in the show."

James said, "Pairno?"

"Offstage, my real name is Mark. I named myself Pernod because it's fake Absinthe. That's me, all over; drugs and artifice." He bent down and kissed Seth, hugged him, and all six feet of him sauntered out of the restaurant.

Seth sniffed and dabbed his eyes with his napkin. "goddammit," he said, "There goes Lady Pernod, my last friend. He's my boyfriend, too, or was. I'm not sure, now."

"So," Seth said, "what are you doing in this hell hole of a city?"

"We're on a mission to find a horse," Blake answered. "Next stop is Fort Worth. There's a ranch there we need to visit."

The waiter brought their orders, and the table was silent as they ate. Soon, without looking up from his Eggs Benedict, Seth said, "I would never ask this if I weren't in such a bind, but is there any chance you could give me a ride to Fort Worth? I have some friends there who can help me out. I would owe you forever."

James spoke before Blake could answer. "Of course we will. It's not very far, is it? Anyway, Blake might like someone to talk to for a change instead of an old fart like me." He winked at Blake, and Blake rolled his eyes.

"I don't have a lot of stuff, but there's too much for hitchhiking. Thank you so much!" He stood and went to

James and hugged him. James smiled, glanced at Blake, and shrugged.

Madame Psyche had lied. She came toward Blake's car, the trunk lid open, trailed by a bellboy and a luggage cart. Somehow, they crammed her luggage into the trunk: suitcases, makeup cases, gowns in hanging bags, a duffle bag, and a ukulele case. There was barely room in the back seat to fit the rest. "We'll be fine," James said, seeing Blake's perturbed expression.

Seth climbed into the back seat, and Blake, still outside at the trunk with James, said, "If you're doing this for the reason I assume you are, I'm not interested, okay? I don't go for drag queens."

"When you were little, you refused to eat dates. Said they looked like monkey poop. One day, I bribed you into eating one. Last time I looked in your refrigerator, you had a big bag of them; get my drift?"

"Okay, but they were Medjool. That doesn't count."

"A date's a date."

"Get in the car, Dad."

"You might thank me later."

"Dates in my refrigerator? Strange what you can remember."

They drove onto the interstate, and Seth leaned forward and looked from James to Blake, saying, "You two are so handsome. James, where'd you get those blue eyes? I'll bet they can stop people in their tracks. I can't decide who to hit on first."

It was only an hour's drive to Fort Worth, but Blake pushed the car past the speed limit.

CHAPTER 7

We're Not In Florida Anymore

It was noon when the men reached Fort Worth. The drive might have been as boring as the landscape if not for Seth's fondness of hearing himself talk. Blake listened to his story while James napped.

"When I'm not doing drag, I'm doing hair in St. Louis, and I take some art classes, too," he said. "I've got a big clientele there, but I love performing and traveling, so I have the best of both worlds. It's fun meeting people, and when I saw you and your dad at the show, I knew I'd like you; I'm psychic that way. Did you know a lot of hairstylists are clairvoyant? They say it comes from playing with people's hair and being so close to their minds so much. I believe it; hair's like antennas. Too bad we don't have more time together; I'd give you both a reading as a thank you for the ride."

Blake said, "That might be fun. Maybe over lunch? I'm getting hungry." He shook his dad's shoulder to wake him, and James opened his eyes. He could see that his father didn't recognize him. James turned away and looked out the window. "Dad, are you ready for something to eat? How about some barbecue? I bet there's some good places along the road here."

James smiled and said, "Okay, I love barbecue. My son used to take me out for it back in Florida. We're not in Florida now, are we?"

"Dad," Blake said, emphasizing the word, "We're in

Texas, on the way to find out where your horse ended up, remember?"

James glanced at the back seat and said, "Who's that fella back there?

Seth spoke up and reached over the seat to shake James's hand, who looked at him with suspicion, but smiled and said, "Oh, I remember you. Didn't you cut my hair once?"

"No, we all look the same," Seth answered, "and I'd remember a good-looking man like yourself."

James looked at Blake and said, "What is he, a Nancy boy?"

Seth laughed. "I haven't heard that one in a long time. No, I'm just your garden variety queer drag queen."

"Well, you be careful out there. There's some mean people in this world."

Blake parked the car in front of a roadside eatery with a sign advertising "Barbecued Brisket, $4.99 All You Can Eat!"

The food was delicious, and as they ate, Seth talked again. "James, I'll bet you've got stories to tell."

"Well, I ought to. I'm as old as God. Not sure what I remember, though. Sometimes my memories are like dreams you wake up in the middle of, before the end."

"Well, don't worry. I believe that if you live something, if it's part of your past, even if you die or forget things, your thoughts and all of your life go on as some kind of energy, and someday they come back to someone. It's hard to explain, but I've seen it a lot, like movies that had things in them I swear were about me, things I never told anyone about. I've wondered if that memory got too big for me and had to spread out to the universe, you know what I mean? And some writer's mind caught it while he slept or got stoned, and he put it in his movie script."

Seth paused and looked at James, who was staring at him with suspicion. He looked at Blake and said, "This son of a bitch is crazy," and returned to his brisket.

"Well, I've heard that before," Seth said. "It might surprise you to know what I can see about you two. But I'm not going into that because some things are meant to be left where they are." He took a bite from his biscuit and said, "At least for now," and glanced at Blake.

Blake thought, *Dad might be right about this guy,* then said, "So, when are you going to let us in on these secrets? Which one of us is the axe murderer?"

Seth narrowed his eyes and looked at Blake. "Never, not with that attitude."

"Sorry, Seth, I'm skeptical about those kinds of things. No offense to you, I just think most of that stuff is superstition, like religion."

"It exists no matter what you think. I know you're going through something you don't understand."

Blake put his fork down, leaned back in his chair, and stared at Seth. "Okay, I'll bite. Why do you say that? "

"I'll explain it sometime. Not here; not now."

Seth lit a cigarette and ordered a beer from the passing waitress. "Y'all don't mind, do you? Sometimes when I talk about this stuff and need something to bring me back to earth, a little alcohol always helps." He held out the pack of cigarettes and said, "Anyone want one of these?"

James shook his head and said, "I wonder if they've got any cigars?"

Blake took a cigarette and said, "I'm screwing up my job of quitting, but what the hell?" He paid the bill at the cash register and bought his dad the best brand of cigar they had.

They smoked while Seth drank his beer and thought about moths and memories, and that he should just shut up. These people were strangers, and something was happening to them that they didn't understand. He believed in fate, that most things happen for a reason, and he was meant to meet them.

James said, "Order me some more sweet tea; I'm going to the men's room. You boys are getting weird."

Blake needed the men's room too, and met his father on his way out. He had seen Blake looking at Seth and said, "Just imagine what you'd save on haircuts."

Blake had to admit that Seth was very attractive. He looked beautiful in drag, so it made sense that he'd be good-looking without his costume. Even with no makeup, his skin was smooth and unblemished, and his eyes were striking, even without mascara. Blake caught himself. *Don't go there. A psychic drag queen? Really?*

Blake reached into his jacket and brought out the postcard Jordan had given him in Mobile. He stopped the waitress and showed her the return address. "Ever hear of this place? Do you know if the ranch is still in operation?"

She laughed and drawled, "No, but it sure looks like fun for somebody. You boys don't seem the type." She handed it back to Blake and said, "Go ask that fella behind the counter. He owns this place, and he's been around Fort Worth for centuries; he can help you out."

Blake approached the man, introduced himself, and showed him the postcard. "We're trying to find this ranch, and we're hoping it still exists. My father had a horse a long time ago, and we think he might have ended up there. My dad wants to find out what became of him."

"I understand," the man said. "I had horses when I was a kid, too. You get attached to them. I know this place; my friends and I used to go down there to ride sometimes," he said and winked at Blake.

"That's what we called it, anyway, until my wife found out what we were really up to. We got divorced over it. Back then, people weren't as open-minded as they are now."

"Is it still there?" Blake asked, hoping he'd have good news for his dad.

"I haven't been down that way in years, but the last time I drove by it was still standing. It didn't look open for business; politics kind of screwed things up for places like that. I'm a Christian and all, but I don't understand why some busybodies need to stick their noses into other people's doings." He looked toward Blake's table, and Seth was holding James's hand and staring at his palm. "You boys gypsies or something?"

"No, sir," Blake answered, "That's my dad and an entertainer friend of ours. Like I said, we're just on our way to find out about a horse. We'll just be passing through."

"Oh, okay, just curious." He glanced at the table again. "Here, let me draw you a little map. It's not hard to find, but a lot of the roads look the same. It's easy to get turned around."

He copied the address from the postcard and looked at the photo again. "You know, that pretty girl on the fence is the owner's daughter. She's getting up in age now. I'm sure she's still alive. She worked with the horses out there; she'll know what happened to yours. What was his name?"

"Chief," Blake answered.

"Chief..." The man stared upward and pursed his lips. "Yes, there was a horse out there named Chief. I used to ride him. Everybody wanted to. He was special. A palomino?"

"Yes, a big, beautiful palomino that my dad got from an Indian chief in Florida."

"Well, that must've been your horse, then. Small world, huh?"

"Thanks so much for your help. We're anxious to get there, so we'd better take off."

As Blake turned to go, the man touched his arm and said, "If you come back this way, I'd sure like to know what she tells you. You see, the girl on the fence is the woman I was cheating with. What can I say? We all do stupid things sometimes. Here, don't forget your map."

Blake took the paper, turned away, and the man said, "Wait, there's a bug on your back." He touched Blake's shoulder and cupped his hands, opened the side door, and watched something flutter into the hot air outside. "Some kind of moth."

Blake returned to their table. "I'm pretty sure I got what we needed from that man. We need to drive south now.

Seth, do you want us to try and get you to your friend's place? They're here in Fort Worth?"

Seth said, "Hell no, are you kidding me? I can't bail now; I want to see what happens." Blake felt a slight tingle of happiness at Seth's answer.

They drove southwest into the prairie, following the man's scrawls on the napkin. They'd been driving for over an hour through the open, bleak landscape, crossed by one empty road after another, almost vacant of cars. Blake imagined the sky growing dark with storm clouds, and a giant tornado dropping down and racing toward them, picking up trees and cows and barns and children trying to get home. He'd been terrified of twisters as long as he could remember, which he blamed on seeing "The Wizard of Oz" as a child on his grandmother's black and white television.

He was tired of driving, and Seth and his father were napping, groggy from their lunch, so he let his daydream take over, and again stood in a field of wildflowers, and the air was hot and humid, and the sky grew dark with clouds. In the distance, a white, two-story farmhouse stood out, desolate and glowing against the gray sky. He ran toward it as fast as his short legs would carry him.

The storm growled like a monster behind him, and he screamed into the wind. He held a stick that had a net on the end. He dropped it and tried to run faster, but fell, and the wind began pushing and rolling him through the dead grass, and the air filled with flowers and leaves rushing by him like frightened birds. The world was as black as a moonless night. He joined the flowers pirouetting up into the vortex of the gigantic, dirty spiral, and he screamed again, trying to be heard above the roar.

"Mama!"

James and Seth jumped in their sleep, woke up, and looked around as if there'd been an accident. Blake parked on the side of the road and walked into the open field.

James said, "That's a good idea. I need a whiz, too."

He joined Blake.

"So, what happened, son? What's all the screaming about?"

"I don't know, Dad. I might be losing my mind."

"Please don't. One nut case in the family is enough. Anything I can do?"

Blake shook his head. "Something's going on, but I don't understand what. Maybe I just need a break from driving. Sometimes I daydream, but this was a terrible nightmare."

Seth joined them nearby and started urinating on the grass. He looked over at Blake and said, "Oh my, I assumed this is the reason we came out here."

Blake said, "Welcome to the club. Dad and I are pros at this."

He didn't stop himself from taking a glance at what filled Seth's hand, and James whispered, "Wonder how he hides that thing?" Blake chuckled, unzipped, and joined the party.

A few miles further on, what appeared to be a faded billboard stood alone in the wilderness on the seldom-used road. As they got closer, James sat up straight, rolled down his window for a clearer view, and said, "Slow down. There's bugs out here." Blake lifted his foot off the gas. The car stopped fifty yards from the sign, and James jumped out of the car and walked toward it. Blake followed and stopped in front of him and looked into his eyes. He feared James was having an early sundowning episode.

"You okay, Dad?" He looked for signs that James might be disoriented or agitated. He hadn't looked at the billboard behind him.

"Dammit, look!" James took Blake's shoulders and turned him around to face the tattered sign.

"Oh, shit!" Blake said and smiled at his dad.

CHAPTER 8

Going To See a Woman About a Horse

"I see, Dad, kind of." All the colors on the torn paper had faded, but enough of the image remained to see that it was the same artwork as the postcard. The barn, the fence, and flowers in the background had survived, along with the young woman wearing a short dress and thigh boots. She sat on a big, blonde horse whose mane blew in the wind as it reared into the Texas sky. The sign read, "Welcome to Annabelle Ranch, the Most Fun You'll Have In the County!"

"Oh fuck! Dad?" Blake said, the truth dawning on him.

"Yep, that's Chief. It is. That's my Chief, dammit!"

They drove on until they saw the ranch in the distance, and even from a mile away, knew it had seen better days. The fences along the road were of no use anymore, and the barn had lost part of its sides. Blake recognized the main house from the picture on the postcard. They rolled up to the front porch.

A woman opened the screen door and said, "Can I help you, boys? Are you lost?"

Blake said, "No, ma'am, we came out here to see someone about a horse. You might be the person we need to talk to."

"We don't keep horses here anymore," she said. "This place hasn't been open for business in a coon's age, not since the tornado."

"We're interested in a horse named Chief you used to keep here."

The woman's expression changed; she stopped smiling and said, "Y'all better come inside. I bet you're thirsty. Come on in, I'll get you a beer."

The parlor was cool and in shadows. They sat in big overstuffed chairs covered in wagon wheel print fabric. An enormous buffalo head hung over the fireplace. The woman brought the beers and settled herself into a rocking chair by the hearth. The lady seemed as old as James, but one could see she had once been a beauty. Her skin was barely lined, but her bright eyes had a sadness in them that made Blake wonder what put it there.

She looked at Blake and said, "So, what's your name, son?"

"Blake, and this is my father, James, and Seth is a friend of ours from Dallas."

She paused, looking from one man to the other, estimating their intentions. "Okay, Chief. What do you want to know about him?"

James spoke first. "He was my horse when I was a kid. I don't know how he got here; I don't remember much of anything anymore, but I'm sure that's Chief on that sign back there on the road. This is my son here. He knows more than I do because he's still got a working brain."

Blake said, "We've been on a trip trying to find out where Chief ended up. My dad wants to find out before..." he paused and looked at the woman, "While he's still able to travel."

"I understand," the woman said. "By the way, my name's Helen. That's me on the billboard. My father hoped it would bring him business if he pimped my image like that. Of course, that gorgeous horse didn't hurt the profits, either. Chief was the most beautiful horse we'd ever had here. It seemed to work; this ranch became quite the place to be back in its day."

"Did Chief die here?" James said.

"Oh, no. People stopped coming out here because the

law started cracking down on places like this. They knew men didn't come here to ride horses but for the backroom stuff going on. The church leaders got their panties in a wad since a lot of our customers belonged to their congregations.

"What we did wasn't legal, but nobody cared until the preachers started ranting in their pulpits about going to hell, and this place being the work of the devil. We were open on Sundays; that really pissed the preachers off. Their bottom lines dwindled; the offering plates started looking awfully empty. Even so, some of our best customers were deacons and preachers, but they always waited 'til after church."

She lit a cigarette, coughed into a Kleenex, and said, "In case you're wondering, I was never one of the working ladies. My father would have killed me. My job was taking care of the horses, not the men. But I loved doing it, and I adored Chief. I hope that makes you feel better, James. You said James, right?"

"Yes, ma'am, and I'm glad you took good care of him. But if he didn't live the rest of his life here, what happened to him after that?"

"We shut the place down rather than put up with raids and paying off the cops; we couldn't afford that. We tried to turn it into a real dude ranch, but our reputation put people off. The wives didn't want their husbands out here; they didn't believe we'd gone straight. And the tourists stayed closer to Dallas and Fort Worth; there were new places there that were a lot nicer than this one. That's where Chief went, to one of them."

Seth said, "Any idea which ranch that was?"

"Well, we still owed money to the man who sold Chief to us. I think he was from Alabama; he came here a few times to ride Chief and have some fun, too. Even brought his little boy once; I watched him while his dad rode the horses, ha! He sold Chief to his friend, who opened a place in Fort Worth. Anyway, that man paid off Chief for us and gave a small fortune to the man from Mobile. It was all kind of hush-hush. People said it was someone famous, but I never knew who. I think Sean knew, but he wouldn't talk about it, like it was a big secret."

"We'd sure like to know about that ranch in Fort Worth. Would the man who gave us directions remember?"

"Who was that? What was his name?" Helen asked.

"I didn't think to ask his name. He owns a brisket restaurant in Fort Worth on the main highway into town, and knows you; said you were the owner's daughter, and that's your picture on the postcard," Blake said.

"That's Sean Murphy. I haven't seen him in years. We used to date when I was young. I still have his phone number, if you want it; that would save you a trip up there unless you're headed back that way."

Blake said, "He told me about his wife and the divorce. I hope he didn't talk out of school. It's none of my business."

"Don't worry. Everybody knew about us after the tornado. We couldn't hide it after that."

Seth said, "What about the tornado? What happened?" He looked at Blake as he said it.

"I wasn't able to talk about it for a long time. I shut down afterward. My father put me in a sanitarium in Dallas for a couple of years; I was that bad. But I'm okay now. I can talk about it some, but don't ask me a lot of questions, okay?"

Everyone was silent, not knowing what to say, and waited for Helen to continue her story.

"You see, Sean was married. I was too young to care about all the trouble that could cause. He had a child, a little girl. She was seven years old, and sometimes he'd bring her out here with him so his wife wouldn't get suspicious."

Helen went to the kitchen and brought back more beers. "You might need these when I tell you the rest of the story." She placed her sun-browned hands in her lap and studied them. "When Sean would bring his daughter out here, we'd get one of the girls to watch her so he and I could wander off somewhere alone. He'd tell her he was just going for a ride on Chief, the star horse. He'd get Chief saddled up and ride to where his daughter could see him, then ride around to the back of the house and sneak in to be with me."

She looked at the men and took a deep breath. "One time, while we were being frisky in a back room, it looked like it was going to storm, so we got out of bed and went to find the whore who was babysitting for us, and there she was on the front porch with a customer's hand up her skirt. I screamed at her, 'Where's the girl?' and she laughed and said, 'She's all right, she's just out there in the field trying to catch a butterfly.'

"We looked out over the prairie and saw a little dot of yellow, far away from the house. We weren't even sure that was her until we made out the butterfly net she was waving in the air."

James spoke up and said, "I hope you fired that whore!"

"Let her finish, Dad," Blake said, and put his hand on his father's knee.

"It just looked like a rainstorm at first, but then the clouds got dark, and in a few minutes, it was almost like nighttime. The horses in the barn were screaming to get out, and the whore and her customer ran inside and hid in a closet. That's when Chief ran up to the porch; he had jumped the corral fence. Some of the other horses ran into the field, away from the storm, but Chief stayed near us, prancing and running in circles, and ran right up to Sean and almost knocked him down with his big head. Sean understood and grabbed Chief's mane and got on him, bareback, and Chief took off like lightning into the field toward the little girl. I ran after them, but they were way ahead of me.

"The twister was growling, forming over us. The clouds were whirling, and the hail came down hard and hit me, and I thought I'd die, it was so painful. We screamed at the little girl to run to us, but she couldn't move in that wind."

Blake looked at Seth; he had tears running down his

face and was nodding as if he already knew the story. Helen was choking back tears, too, and James took her hand. She grabbed it and held on as if she'd disappear if he let go.

"The goddamn thing came out of the sky, roaring and howling like a live animal or some monster from your worst nightmare. It came down right on top of the girl, who was screaming for her mother. Chief was taking Sean right toward her, but she disappeared into the dirty wind and rain before they could get to her. We saw her yellow dress in flashes of lightning, flying higher and higher until it disappeared up in the tornado." Helen was sobbing, and James squeezed her hand even tighter.

"The twister moved off into the distance, then shrank to nothing and disappeared. We ran further into the field, screaming her name, 'Annabelle, Annabelle' but of course there was no answer. We never found her, not the butterfly net or her body." She looked up, across the room, and out of the windows. "She was gone, just like that. She just flew away, like a little yellow bird."

She looked at Blake and said, "You, know, you never get over something like that. It eats you alive." She drank from her beer, shook her head, and looked in silence out toward the prairie.

"Anyway, a few weeks later, somebody in the next county found her little yellow dress in a tree, with not even a tear in it.

"Chief wasn't the same after that. He just seemed sad and kind of broken, like the rest of us. He wanted to save that little girl, but even he couldn't outrun a tornado." The room became silent; they heard a train's horn blowing somewhere miles away on the prairie.

"You named the ranch after her?" Blake said.

"No, just the opposite. Sean talked his wife into naming her Annabelle, after the ranch. I'll never understand why she agreed." Helen stubbed out her cigarette and took a long drink of her beer. "My father just liked the name

Annabelle, so that's what he called the ranch. There wasn't any reason that I knew of.

"Sean never came out here again; it hurt him too much to remember. A reporter showed up and talked to the whore, who paid her for her story. It was unbelievable that the bitch took the money. She told him everything except what she was up to when the storm came. That's why Sean's wife divorced him. Not because of me, but because she blamed him for Annabelle's death." Helen looked up from her hands and said, "Sean's wife never got over it. She blamed herself for letting Annabelle come here with Sean that day. A few years later, she killed herself, right out there in that field. People said her heart just couldn't take that much pain."

James said, "Chief tried to save that little girl like he saved me once."

Blake said, "He must have loved Annabelle like he loved you, Dad."

No one spoke. The train blew its horn again; the melancholy sound drifted over the dry prairie like the long mourning cries of a lonely ghost. Seth tried to smile at Blake, but it became a look of sweet compassion and understanding as if he understood Blake's fear and confusion; his gift was becoming stronger.

Seth said, "Don't worry; we'll talk soon."

CHAPTER 9

That's What Moths Do

Helen went into her little office behind the fireplace wall and returned with a scrap of paper, gave it to Blake, and said, "Here's Sean's number. He knows more about Chief than I do. I was young, and he didn't talk to me much. That was okay; just being with him made me happy."

She motioned toward her office. "There's a phone in there you can use to call him."

"I'd appreciate that," Blake said. "Can I do it now? We'll go soon, but I need to know where we're going."

Helen said, "Sure, go ahead. If you get Sean on the line, could you tell him something for me?" She paused and looked toward the window. "Tell him I wouldn't mind seeing him if he's ever down this way."

Blake went into the office, dialed the phone, and a voice said, "Murphy's, Sean here."

A few moments later, Blake came out of the office. "Helen, Sean's holding for you; he wants to say hello. Dad, you're not going to believe this."

Helen hesitated, went to her office door, and said, "Y'all shouldn't wait for me if you're in a hurry. This might take a while."

Blake said, "I understand. Thanks for seeing us. You've been a tremendous help."

He held out his hand, but Helen brushed it aside and hugged him. "Drive carefully. Good luck; I hope you find what you're after." She entered her office and closed the door.

Blake wanted to speak, but the sound of Helen weeping stopped him. He whispered, "Come on, you two, let's go. I'll tell you in the car." As Blake left the room, something in the little bookcase by the door caught his eye: *Collected Poems of Edgar Allan Poe.* Only Seth noticed the brown-winged insect dying on the windowsill.

They were driving north, and the daylight was dimming. Blake said, "We'd better spend the night in Fort Worth. We've got a long drive tomorrow."

"Fine," Seth said, "But I don't want to wait to hear what Mr. Murphy told you."

Blake cleared his throat. "Okay, this is the deal. Y'all ready for this?"

Blake glanced at his father to make sure he was awake. "You remember that letter Jordan in Mobile had? The one to his dad from AM?"

Seth said, "Yes, we remember. So?"

"Well, AM was none other than," he paused... "Audie Murphy!"

Round-eyed and staring, Seth said, "And we're supposed to know who that is?"

James said, "Are you kidding? Was he pulling your leg?"

"I don't believe so. Sean told me that he's Audie Murphy's cousin. Audie Murphy had lots of relatives, and Sean is one of them."

"What does that have to do with anything?"

"Jordan in Mobile's father was a friend of Audie Murphy's and sold him a horse; that horse was Chief. Audie bought Chief from Jordan's dad and paid the balance that Helen's dad owed, too."

Blake looked at James and waited for his reaction. James was staring at him, squinting, his mouth open, trying to make sense of it. Blake stayed quiet until his father blurted out, "You mean Audie Murphy ended up with my Chief?"

"Yes, Dad. How do you feel about that?"

James bowed his head and began to cry. Blake reached out with one hand, the other on the steering wheel, and squeezed his father's shoulder. James leaned forward, and Blake patted his back. "Isn't that great, Dad? Aren't you happy for him? How many horses got to be ridden by Audie Murphy?"

From the back seat, Seth yelled, "Who the fuck is Audie Murphy? Will someone please tell me?"

Blake said, "You don't know who he was? He was majorly famous. Cowboy movies, a big war hero, a country music composer, a huge star, and he owned ranches and horses. I can't believe you don't know who he was. He was from Texas, this area."

"Excuse me; I'm not just an ignorant drag queen. Maybe I'm not old enough."

James sat up straight and said, "My Chief. Everybody said he was so beautiful he should be in the movies."

"He might have been in movies. Audie Murphy had a studio, I think. Tomorrow we'll drive to his old ranch and talk to the people there who might remember Audie and Chief. Won't that be something, Dad? Maybe they know what happened to him."

"Audie Murphy," James whispered. "I admired him so much. He was a real hero in the war. A little guy, too, but that didn't faze him. He killed lots of Germans and saved a lot of lives. They don't make men like that anymore. My Chief..." His voice faded, and he got comfortable and quickly fell asleep, drained and happy.

Blake said, "Oh shit. Seth, are you psychic enough to tell me where to find a gas station? Dammit, I meant to fill up yesterday. We're going to need gas very soon."

They were near the city's outskirts, but civilization was still distant. Seth stared at the horizon and saw a neon glow on the darkening plain. "Try over there, Blake; that might be one."

Blake turned onto the next road and drove toward the light. The road joined a larger one and soon became a busy highway. There were bright letters ahead spelling "Motel and Restaurant, Trucks and Bikers Welcome."

"What about cars and queers?" Seth laughed.

"Keep your wrists straight. We might end up staying the night."

James pumped gas while Blake went into the restaurant, which also served as the motel office. The only room available had king beds; Blake didn't want to drive to Fort Worth in the dark, so he paid for the room, parked the car in front of it, and met Seth and James in the restaurant, seated and reading menus. The jukebox was playing a country song; "Shutters and Boards". Seth said, "I hope the mattress isn't as awful as that song."

James glared at him and said, "Audie Murphy wrote that song. Show some respect."

The room looked clean but had a musty smell left by years of travelers. Its decor was original to its beginnings, and Blake enjoyed seeing that the design was preserved, not from love, but from economy. The bathroom was a treasure, with pink and black tile and mint green fixtures. He wondered how anyone ever liked it, even though someday it would probably be in style again.

Seth offered to get a rollaway bed. James said, "Don't do that. Those things are horrible. These beds are huge and you two are skinny. Don't be prudes."

He winked at Blake, who looked at him and mouthed, "I'll get you."

"I don't mind sharing," Seth said and closed the bathroom door before Blake could answer.

James was asleep when Blake got into bed and turned his back toward Seth, who said, "Thanks for letting me come along with you; I needed this. I'll tell you about it sometime."

"Don't mention it. I haven't minded you coming along, you're not bad company."

"I guess that's supposed to make me feel better," Seth laughed.

Blake turned over and faced Seth. "Can we talk now? I'm worried; I don't understand these crazy things that have been happening to me, the dreams and visions. What do I make of them? I dream something and later on find out it happened to somebody else. It seems like it's old hat to you."

Seth whispered, "It is. I've been where you are. Not the same, but close. But I wasn't afraid, because I welcome things like that. It's a gift, and I'm trying to make the best of it. You should, too."

"It feels more like a curse. I don't enjoy having nightmares in the daytime when I'm wide awake. Pleasant dreams are fine, but getting sucked into a tornado is not." Blake was looking at Seth's face, barely visible in the dark room. He wanted to touch it, but held back the urge.

Seth took Blake's hand and held it to his cheek. "There. I don't bite. You're better now, aren't you?"

"A little. I want to learn how to turn it off."

"When you realize what it can do, you won't want to. You can learn to control it, though," Seth was still holding Blake's hand, tracing circles in his palm with his fingers.

"I want nothing to do with it," Blake said, aware that he was enjoying what Seth was doing. "You'd better stop that. I haven't been with anyone in ages, and now's not a good time."

"Sorry. I can't help wanting to be physical with someone when I'm this attracted to them."

"Let's sleep now," Blake said and turned over, away from Seth.

Seth touched Blake's shoulder. "Listen, have you seen those pictures that if you learn how to stare at them right, things pop out in three dimensions and you can't figure out how that happens? You look away, then look again, and it's back to normal? If you do it often enough, it will happen in seconds instead of minutes? Well, it's like that. The point is, you can make it go away, or come back if that's what you want. But it takes practice."

Blake muttered, "Why would I want it? Life's weird enough as it is."

Seth moved closer to Blake's ear and whispered, "You've got something I've never seen; I don't have it, not like you, anyway. It's because your dad is forgetting his life; you're a part of that."

"But why was I getting Helen's memories, and Sean Murphy's? Aren't they supposed to be from people I care for, or at least know?"

"Because you're on this trip to learn about Chief's life. Those memories might have come from him. Maybe he wants you to know. That was a big event for him."

"Memories from a horse? Oh, come on!"

"Okay, that's enough for now. You'll get it, eventually. I'll let you sleep."

"Thanks. I know you mean well, and I do need to sleep on it. Goodnight."

Hours later, Blake got up to use the bathroom and entered it without turning on the light. He could see the commode by the glow of the wall light outside the shower window. He looked into his father's room on his way back to bed and saw that his father wasn't there.

Blake turned on the bedside lamp and said, "Shit!" Seth rolled over, half-opened his eyes, and said, "What is it?"

"Dad's not here." He opened the door and looked outside to the parking lot, then the walkway. James was standing a half dozen doors down under one of the light fixtures, staring up at it. Blake ran to him.

"Hi, Dad. Are you all right?" James didn't move or even glance at Blake, but kept staring at the yellow light bulb. "Come back inside, okay? It's chilly out here."

James looked at him. His eyes were wide open, and he looked afraid. "These things here; what are they?"

"It's only a light bulb, Dad. Come on back inside and

let's go to sleep."

James pointed at the light. "No, these things flying around. They woke me up." There were moths, many of them, circling and diving at the bright glow from the glass shade. Some were hitting it, trying to reach the bulb inside, and falling to the concrete. "They're killing themselves. Why are they doing that, mister?"

"That's what moths do. They're not very smart. Let's go back to the room." Blake was at a loss for how to handle the situation. His mother had been through this many times, but he hadn't and didn't know how to bring his dad back to reality.

"I'm not going anywhere with you. I don't know you, and you might be going to rob me. Where is my wife? She better not be somewhere with somebody. Can you find her for me, please?"

He looked back up at the moths. "These damn things were all over me, on my face and everywhere. Can you tell my wife I need her?"

Blake stood frozen in place, unable to help. "Let me talk to him," Seth said, now standing behind him. He gently pushed Blake aside and said, "Hi, James. You might not remember me. I'm a friend of your son. Let's go inside and see if we can figure this out."

He touched James's arm, and James smiled and said, "That's better." They walked carefully together to their room, Seth helped him into bed, and in moments he was snoring.

He and Blake got into their bed, and Seth pressed his body into Blake's back and put his arm over him. "Don't freak out. A little spooning never hurt anybody." Blake pushed himself closer to Seth, and soon they were sleeping and dreaming together of flowers and beautiful men.

The next morning, Blake phoned his mother at his aunt's house. Evelyn answered. "Hi, Aunt Evelyn, it's Blake. Is my mother handy?" Blake heard the clunk as she put the receiver down without saying a word.

"Nice talking to you, Auntie," he said, as loudly as he could. His mother spoke into the phone, "Hi, honey, how's Dad? Y'all having a good time?"

"Better than you are, I'd wager," Blake answered.

"She's nicer than she used to be. I think she's afraid she might die soon, so she'd better change her ways, so Jesus will like her," she said, laughing. "Anyway, how are things going? Where are y'all now?"

"We're almost to Fort Worth. Dad's okay, I guess, but he had an episode last night. He went outside at four o'clock this morning and I found him in the hallway. He's okay now, but I didn't know what to do."

"I'm sorry; it's scary at first. Just talk to him nicely and tell him he's safe, and he'll usually calm down. But you'd better plan on coming home soon. It might be time for him to go someplace where they can look after him better. I'll admit it's been nice to not have that burden for a while, and I'm not sure I can do it anymore."

"Mom, you've given it your best shot. Dad would understand."

"Thanks. I'm just not sure I'm ready."

"He was asking where you were. Can you say hello to him?"

"Sure, if it won't upset him, put him on."

James was sitting on his bed next to Blake. "Someone wants to talk to you, Dad."

He handed James the receiver. "Who is this?" he said.

Mary answered, "It's your wife, Mary. How are you, honey?"

"I'm doing fine. Your little boy is taking good care of me. Do you have enough money?"

James handed the phone to Blake. "We'll call you again in a couple of days. I'm not sure yet when we'll be home. It's been a good trip. Good luck with Evelyn. Give her a big kiss for me." Seth heard Mary laughing on the phone speaker across the room.

He hung up and dialed the number Sean Murphy had given him for the Fort Worth ranch. A man answered, and Blake explained their mission. "We're trying to find out where Chief ended up."

The man on the phone said, "I don't remember Chief; I wasn't born yet, but my father talked a lot about him. If you can give me a little while, I'll see if I can find something in my dad's records. He wrote everything down."

Seth took James to the motel restaurant for breakfast while Blake waited for the call. They'd just gotten their food when Blake sat down at the table.

"Dad, can you stand some more driving? Chief went farther away than Helen thought."

Seth looked alarmed. "How far? I'd better not skip work much longer. I could catch up with my drag company; they're doing two weeks in Phoenix. So, what's up now?"

"This might work out for you. I found out Chief was at a ranch in Vail, Arizona, just south of Tucson."

James was eating his eggs and looking perplexed. "I don't mind going. What else have I got to do?"

Blake picked up a map from the office, and Seth volunteered to drive so Blake could rest. He'd made himself as comfortable as he could, lying on the back seat, his head on Seth's bags, and fell asleep right away. Seth drove onto the highway, hoping to get halfway to Vail and stop in Odessa for the night. It was a long drive to Tucson, and Blake didn't want to exhaust his father.

The sound of squealing brakes and tires struggling to stop awakened Blake. He tried to sit up, but the car rolled onto its side, the door opened, and he tumbled out into the grass. He lay on the ground, unable to move. There were blue wildflowers around him, and someone called his name, and he thought, *Is this how I die?*

CHAPTER 10

Odessa is a Drag

"Blake! Wake up, man, you're having a nightmare," Seth yelled. Blake opened his eyes and looked at him. "It was another one, wasn't it?" Seth said, stopping the car on the grassy shoulder.

"They're getting more vivid each time, and scary. I don't like this," Blake answered.

James was staring at Blake, unsure of what had happened; his eyes were wide, and he looked confused. Blake said, "It's okay, Dad. It was just a bad dream. Can you hand me that water bottle up there?"

"Want me to take over, Seth? I'm good now."

They agreed to switch places, but James stopped them and said, "Let me get back there. I could use a rest myself. You two can talk. Then you can tell me where the hell we are."

Driving on toward Odessa, Blake talked about his dream. "I was in a car and there was an accident; the car left the road and rolled into a field and turned over on its side, and I went flying out the door. I could see the sky before I landed in the grass. There were flowers and cow dung around me. I think we busted through a fence. I tried to get up, but my head was hurting, so I just lay there until I heard voices, and then you woke me."

"Sorry, you were yelling something and crying like a kid. It was frightening."

James raised himself, looked over the front seat, and

said, "That happened to me once. I was only five or so, and Daddy was driving us to Alabama. Me and my brothers were in the back of the truck; people used to do that back then. A deer ran in front of the truck, but the brakes were old, and it hit the deer and then swerved through the fence and threw us out onto the grass. We were okay, but it scared Mother to death. That was the last time we rode in the truck bed."

Seth looked at Blake. "We kinda knew about that, didn't we?"

James lay on the seat and was soon snoring. "Want to relax after that dream, Blake? Anything I can do to help calm you down?" Seth smiled and rubbed Blake's thigh.

"Dad is in the back seat, for god's sake!" Blake laughed and took Seth's hand and placed it on the seat next to him.

"He's dead to the world." His hand went back to Blake's leg and slid up the denim to his growing crotch. Blake ignored it, keeping his eyes on the road and his hands firmly on the steering wheel.

Blake felt Seth's fingers on him as they unzipped his jeans and found their way inside his pants, freeing his penis. The cool air on it felt exquisite and the freedom of it welcome, and Seth's hand did its work, and in moments it was over and Seth was looking for a Kleenex in the glove box.

"I think that was long overdue. You should take better care of yourself."

The men arrived in Odessa at sunset, checked into a motel, then went to a 1950s-style diner across the street. The walls were decorated with cowboy memorabilia and bull's horns, and the waitress was dressed in a gaudy, sequined cowgirl costume. Sitting in a booth by a plate glass window, they looked at framed photos of famous people who had visited there before. James studied them and said, "Look! There's Audie Murphy! Wonder if he came through here with Chief. Wouldn't that be something if Chief was in a trailer right here in the parking lot?"

"It could have happened, Dad." James smiled and stared out the window, and while they ate, the street became crowded with souped-up cars, hot rods, and fancy trucks driving up and down the street past them like a two-way parade. The drivers waved to each other, sometimes stopping to pick up girls on the side of the road. "This must be the place to go on a Friday night. We'd better finish up before the drag races start so we can make it across the road alive."

Despite the noise of the cars and voices outside, they slept well. Seth placed his arm around Blake's waist, and Blake let it stay. During the night, Blake turned over and kissed Seth on the cheek and smiled.

Blake had been asleep for a while when Seth shook his shoulder and said, "Blake, wake up; your father's gone."

He sat up, turned on the light, and said, "Fuck, not again," pulled on his clothes, and went to check the bathroom, then ran out the front door. Seth grabbed a bathrobe and went outside, and tried to see Blake in the street, still busy with cars and people. He spotted him walking away and heard him calling James's name, then began to run.

Blake pushed his way through the circle of people in the middle of the pavement and saw his father sitting on the asphalt, crying and clutching his knee. There was blood running down his arm, his pajama bottoms were torn, and he was missing a shoe.

He knelt beside his father and said, "It's okay, Dad, I'm here. Don't worry, you'll be fine." He could hear an ambulance approaching, and people yelling, "Get back, let them through," and Blake took his father's hand.

James said, "Where's my wife? What is happening to me? Where the hell am I?"

A young man knelt beside Blake and said, "He just walked in front of a car. I tried to grab him, but he pulled away and said he had to get to that horse trailer over there. He stepped in front of that Camaro," he said, pointing to a shiny blue Chevrolet.

The driver of the Chevy was behind the wheel, shaking his head and talking to someone leaning against his door. He got out and went to Blake, sitting on the pavement.

"I'm sorry. I couldn't help hitting him. He just walked into my car like he didn't see it." He'd been crying. "I hope he'll be okay. My parents will kill me."

"I understand. Don't worry, I know it wasn't your fault. He's got Alzheimer's and wanders sometimes." The medics were lifting James's stretcher into the ambulance when he felt Seth's hand on his back.

"I'm going to go get dressed and I'll meet you at the hospital," Seth said, and turned to leave, then stopped and said, "Blake, look!" He pointed toward the open door of the ambulance, and Blake saw yellow wings fly out from it and lift into the hot air over the street, then disappear into the black sky beyond the street lights.

Blake climbed into the ambulance and sat beside his father while the technicians worked over him. James fought them, shouting for his wife, then for Blake. One medic looked at Blake and said, "His vitals look okay. I think he's just banged up a little. They'll tell you more at the hospital."

Blake understood; he knew his dad was more than just wounded. Things were leaving him, pieces of his life, but they'd soon come back to visit Blake's dreams and take root in his mind; he was beginning to see how this thing worked.

James's doctor was young, empathetic, and professional, and said that James should stay overnight despite his injuries being minor. Blake telephoned his mother to tell her about the accident. "I'll see what the doctor says tomorrow. I guess I'll stay the night with him," Blake said.

Mary said, "You need to forget about this horse trip and get him back home. You don't know what he might do next."

"Maybe so, Mother, but I want to finish this thing," Blake said, trying to get the courage to say, "I need to ask you something about Dad when he was young. I don't imagine he'd tell you this, but did he ever talk about beating up gay guys? He and his friends?"

Mary was silent, but Blake could hear her breathing. "Mom, are you there?"

"I'm sorry. I was sleeping when you called, and this took me by surprise. Why would you ask that?" The tone of her voice changed, and she sounded defensive.

"He said something about it. Not much, but I got the feeling he was trying to confess something."

More silence, then Mary said, "He told me once that when he was in high school, he was with his friends driving around in the country, like kids that age do, and they saw a boy from school walking along the road. Everybody said he was a homosexual. Before Dad knew it, they were running after the poor guy, throwing him on the ground, and yelling for your dad to take the boy's wallet. He said they beat him up, too. Dad has suffered the guilt of that night all his life, but it got worse when you were older and he realized you were gay. I still wonder why he'd tell you about that; he was so ashamed."

"Maybe because he's got dementia and things just come out. Maybe he wants to get it off his chest before he dies. Who knows? Did he say what became of the boy? Was he all right?"

Mary took a deep breath and paused for a few moments. "They hurt him so bad that he was in the hospital for a long time. One of Dad's friends hit the boy in the head with a bat. The kid never came back to school; his parents took him and moved out of town. The thing is, he never told the police, or anyone, who'd done it to him. Your dad said he was afraid they might come for him again."

"Thanks for telling me, Mom. I can't believe Dad did something like that."

"He was young and let his friends push him into it. I think there was whiskey involved, and peer pressure. Try not to hold it against him. He had nothing against gay people.

Dad loves you, and he's suffered for what he did. He's never forgiven himself, and he never wanted you to know about what happened."

Blake hung up the phone and the doctor approached him and said, as if he'd heard his phone call, "You guys don't need to stay. We've got him sedated and he'll sleep all night. We have skilled nurses here in case he needs something. Just leave us a contact number."

Seth drove them to the motel, stopping first to buy a bottle of bourbon. They made drinks and propped themselves up in bed. Blake turned on the television; Seth turned the sound down low so they could talk.

"You saw that butterfly, didn't you?" Seth said.

"Yes, I saw it. I wonder what that one will be. Maybe I'll find out tonight. I hope the next dream will at least be something pleasant." He told Seth about his conversation with Mary.

Seth said, "When you told me about that dream, I was afraid it would be something like that."

"I guess the memories don't censor the truth. I'm not sure I want this to keep happening. There's got to be other things I don't want to know about; private things that Dad wouldn't want me to know."

Seth took Blake's hand and looked at him. "I know it's late, but it might be nice to forget all this for a while. What do you say?"

Blake finished his drink in one gulp and said, "I can't think of a reason not to. It feels like forever since I was with someone. Someday I might tell you why. Takes me a long time to get over things. But tonight I might be ready to let go."

Seth wasted no time, and in moments they were naked and pressing their bodies together, and the night became what Blake had needed for too long.

Blake awoke while Seth was still sleeping and stared at his beautiful features, thinking about possibilities he hadn't considered in years. He called the hospital and whispered to the doctor, so as not to wake Seth.

"He's awake and feeling good, and doesn't remember what happened. He's asking for you and Mary. Is that his wife?"

"Yes, my mother. Will they discharge him today?"

"Someone will have to take care of his arm and leg, cleaning them and changing the dressings. Can you do that?" The doctor's voice sounded doubtful.

"I think so. Maybe someone there could show me how. We need to get on the road as soon as we can."

"Okay, come down here in about an hour. We'll get him ready, and I'll show you what you need to do. He's got medication to take, too. It's important."

Blake showered and dressed before he woke Seth. "I'll go get Dad, and you can stay here and pack. It shouldn't take long."

Seth smiled and said he'd be ready and winked. "Say hi to that hunky doctor for me. I think he liked you."

Blake smiled as he drove to the hospital. The weather was clear and warm; the sky was as blue as he could remember ever having seen it. There were no tornadoes on the horizon and not a butterfly in sight.

The doctor had dismissed James's nurse and was showing Blake the proper way to wrap the bandage on his dad's arm when he said, "So, where's your friend? Is he traveling with you?"

Blake thought the question was a little out of line, but answered, "Yes, we're dropping him off in Phoenix. He's got work there."

"Well, if you come back through here, I'd like to check on your dad's wound, so please stop by. Here's my card." The doctor smiled at Blake, and the implication was clear.

"Thank you. We'll be sure and do that." Seth was right. A doctor; his mother would be thrilled.

They drove west toward Las Cruces and planned to

stop there for the night. The drive wasn't too long, and Blake hoped James could endure it with his wounds. He slept most of the time while Seth and Blake talked in the front seat.

"Every time I've been through New Mexico, I've felt an amazing energy that makes me want to stay forever," Seth said. "It's a magical place."

"This will be my first time. I wonder if I'll feel that, too."

"At the risk of sounding sappy, I thought last night was magical. I know you had to get to your dad this morning, but you kind of rushed out before I could say anything. I thought maybe you felt embarrassed."

Blake put his hand on Seth's knee and said, "It was nice to be with you. I felt so good this morning, like maybe something had let go of me, like maybe I can be happy again and get on with my life. I know you don't understand what I'm talking about, but don't think I didn't love what happened last night."

"Whoever did this to you did a good job of fucking you up, didn't they?"

"There's no one to blame. Something happened, that's all. It was the universe that fucked me up."

Seth put his hand on Blake's leg and closed his eyes. In a few moments, he opened them, and tears were running down his cheeks. "Oh, I am so, so very sorry. I am just so sorry for you. Whatever it was, you didn't deserve it. I hate when bad things happen to good people." Seth sniffed and put his hand on Blake's neck, caressing it softly.

"It was just an accident. I don't believe it had anything to do with me being good or bad. Bad things happen, that's all. None of it makes sense because there's no sense to it."

Seth stared at Blake, unblinking, and Blake kept his eyes looking ahead at the smooth, black highway before them. He gripped the wheel a little tighter and took a deep breath, then breathed out.

"I was driving my sister up to Atlanta to a medical center there. She had a cancer that hardly anyone had heard of, but a hospital in Georgia said they could cure it, so I offered to drive her. She was only twenty-six and still single. My dad said it was because no man could stand her for long, but I loved her and accepted her for what she was. They used to call her feisty, like she enjoyed fighting. She was smart, and talented and she knew her mind and what she could accomplish with it. I was the peacemaker between her and my parents; they just didn't get her. I think she had some mental problems, but back then, people were ashamed of anything like that and tended to ignore the possibility." James coughed, and Blake glanced at the back seat to make sure he was sleeping and not listening to him.

He began speaking again, letting the story come out of him, finally allowing himself to tell someone, after all the time that had passed, about the thing that had left him so wounded, guilty, and void of happiness.

"Dad still calls her a bitch; that's his way of pretending she's alive. He loved her, even though she could be awful to my parents. She tried to be the person they wanted her to be, but she was angry because they hated who she was. It wasn't fair. Mom doesn't talk about her, ever, but I know she hurts."

The landscape was like a beautiful O'Keeffe painting created just for them, and the vast prairie seemed to whisper a welcome to Blake. Mountains in the distance looked like the place he craved: a beautiful and pure high-range home where he could build the life he had dreamed of; a life of clear, crisp air and honest labor.

"I need to stretch my legs," Blake said. He pulled the car onto the shoulder, got out, and began walking into the sand and brush. He stopped and looked back at the car; Seth sat with his head bowed, giving Blake the moment of privacy he knew was needed. Blake sat on the sand and cried uncontrollably, letting relief flow from him out into the open air and toward the peaks in the distance. The warmth of the sand under him felt comforting and brought him back to the present and on into the future, perhaps toward the life he wanted.

Blake opened his eyes and saw a brown lizard on a cactus in front of him, holding a butterfly in its mouth, staring at him as if he were presenting the insect to him as a gift.

He rose and turned toward the car. Seth was walking up to him, and reaching for him, offered a drink from his water bottle. Blake drank and started speaking again. There was more he needed to say, and then he'd be done with it, he hoped, forever.

"It's really hard to tell this story."

Seth touched his arm. "I'm here. Go on."

"We were almost to Atlanta when she started talking some shit, just out of nowhere, about how hard it was to have a fag for a brother. She said she loved me in the same sentence. I tried to ignore her; I'd heard it all before, but she just wanted to fight. She was like that. That's how she communicated. She was worried about her cancer, and that's how she dealt with it. She was being her cruel self when she ordered me to let her out of the car because she needed some fresh air. I said no; it was too dangerous. She started pounding the dashboard with her fists and said, 'Come on, you pussy faggot. Let me out now. I can't breathe in this car.'

"I said, 'Don't talk to me like that. You know I hate that word.'

"She screamed, 'Let me out, dammit!'

"So I pulled over. She got out and came around to my open window, leaned in, and said, 'Little brother, you know I love you. I'm just a bitch, like everybody says. And I don't know why.' She always called me little brother, even though I was older."

Blake drank again from the bottle, looked away from Seth, and said, almost inaudibly, "Then she stepped backward, away from the car, onto the highway, looking at me, crying. I screamed at her to get back inside, but she wouldn't move. I was trying to get my damned seatbelt off when a big truck hit her and, in an instant, she was gone; she just flew away. Just like that."

He turned and looked at Seth, his eyes red and wet, and Seth said, "You couldn't have saved her."

"Maybe not on that highway, but maybe before she got so bad. But even if I could have, she didn't want me to.

"I stopped the car. I always let her have her way, I guess because I loved her."

"And all this time you never loved anyone else, because of what happened?"

"After that, it didn't feel right to be happy."

CHAPTER 11
Fishnet Stockings

"Let me pick the hotel," Seth said as they entered Las Cruces. "After all, this could be our last night together. If I don't make Phoenix soon, I could lose the gig. And I want us to stay someplace memorable." Blake's heart skipped when Seth said, "Last night." He had hoped Seth might change his mind.

He parked, and Seth crossed the street to the Welcome Center and soon returned with hotel brochures. "I hope they show the rates in those places. This trip is costing more than I thought it would," Blake said. "I need to call my clients and tell them I haven't disappeared."

"Don't worry, I can pay my share. Here, check this one out," Seth said, handing the pamphlet to Blake. The cover photos showed a large adobe building with a swimming pool, a Mexican restaurant, and a cute bellboy.

"You said in Dallas you were broke."

Seth giggled. "I lied."

"And the friends in Fort Worth?"

"Lied."

The hotel had a vacancy. Blake sat on one of the king-sized beds and changed the bandage on James's arm. Looking around, he approved of the modern Mexican decor, and the spotless room smelled nice and had a balcony that overlooked the pool.

James winced as Blake cleaned the wound. "You sure are one ugly nurse."

"You're lucky I didn't leave you behind. Don't go wandering off again, okay? My heart can't take any more of that."

"I don't know what you mean," James said. Blake laughed, hoping he was joking, then realized he had no memory of the accident. "Where is this place? Is this a hospital? You better be a doctor!"

Blake felt a mild jolt of panic. *Perhaps Mother's right,* he thought, *and we should wind this trip up soon.*

"It's me, Blake, your son."

"Liar! I don't have a son. What happened to my arm, you son of a bitch?"

Seth came out of the bathroom and knew something was wrong by Blake's expression.

"And who the hell is he? I want my wife and I want to go home."

Seth said, "Could be the drugs. He'll be okay after a night's rest."

Blake pulled a business card from his wallet. "I'm going to call that doctor. This doesn't feel right." He phoned the hospital in Odessa, but the doctor wasn't available. He spoke for a few moments, hung up, and said, "The nurse said pain and the antibiotics could stir up dementia, and we should get him to a hospital."

The front desk gave them directions, and soon James was asleep in a private hospital room a few blocks away. The hotel restaurant served Mexican food, and when they returned, they ordered Tex-Mex platters and drank Dos Equis.

"While I bandaged Dad, I remembered the daydream I had driving away from Dad's old homestead. I was a young guy with a boy, and we had rifles but were more interested in what we had in our pants. It wasn't a daydream, but a memory, and not mine."

Seth put his fork down. "What? You think that was a dad memory?"

"Who else? We'd just left the place in the country where he grew up, and they hunted a lot, and in the vision I was wearing blue jeans, until I pulled them down, and the other boy wore overalls. It was a long time ago. It had to be my dad. And afterward, there was a butterfly in the car with us."

"Well, I'll be damned. The day we met, I had a vibe about James. That might explain why he's so comfortable with the gay thing."

"I wish he could've talked about it. Maybe that's why he defended me and my cousin to Aunt Evelyn when she caught us messing around."

"Most boys experiment with each other sometimes. Those hormones are crazy at that age, then they grow up and never mention it again. Most, anyway."

"When I did it, I was sure I'd go to hell, and thought a hard-on was some kind of medical problem. Nobody explained those things to me, at least no one in the family. They figured we'd just know, like animals do."

"But not do it, right?" Seth laughed. "That hell thing; what a way to screw up a kid."

"It took some time to get past it. Masturbating would bring on a world of guilt."

They wanted some fun and decided to visit a gay bar in town. While Blake showered and changed, Seth called the Phoenix club where his group had begun their run. The manager put Lady Pernod on the phone.

"Nothing was happening in St. Louis, so here I am in Phoenix after all. I need the work, and this is a nice gig. Where the hell are you?"

"Headed your way, but it'll be at least another day. Can you ask them not to give up my spot?"

"Sure, honey, that won't be a problem. We need your pretty face. But how are you? Where are you?"

"I'm in Las Cruces, not too far from Phoenix. That nice couple in Dallas offered me a ride."

"That old man and that hunk in the restaurant? Sounds like an interesting trip."

"We'll catch up when I get there."

They were surprised that Las Cruces had such an impressive gay nightclub. There was an elegant, mirrored restaurant, a Western-themed bar with the biggest disco ball Blake had ever seen, and a huge showroom with a velvet-curtained stage. The show was excellent, and Seth approved. During the last drag performance, he leaned over and whispered in Blake's ear, "Oh my god, that's a friend of mine from St. Louis. We used to perform together." He'd made himself up to be believable as Barbra Streisand and did a perfect impression of her movements, lip-syncing perfectly to "My Man".

"We'll go backstage after the show. I'd love to speak to her."

They squeezed their way through the crowd to go to the smoky dressing room. The performers were changing, and Blake felt he was intruding. Seth pulled him into the room, saying, "Come on, they won't mind. You can see what I go through. Tucking isn't much fun." Seth's friend was removing her makeup. Her wig was on the dressing table, and she wore only lace panties and fishnet stockings. She was muscular, and Blake wondered how she'd appeared so thin and feminine on stage.

"Oh, shit! Miss Madame Psyche! How are you, baby?" The drag queen hugged Seth and glanced at Blake. "What the fuck are you doing in this nasty town? Are you playing here?"

"No, honey. We're going to Phoenix; I've got work there. This is my friend Blake; he's giving me a lift. We met in Dallas; I was in a show there. Blake, this is my old friend Holly Trinity, AKA Jules Cohen."

"So, is Pernod with you? Aren't you together?" She smiled at Blake, then winked at Seth.

"She's in Phoenix doing a show. I'm running a little late,

but they're holding a spot for me."

"Well, it's so nice of this fine man to give you a ride." She narrowed her eyes and looked at Seth. "I guess you'll get to introduce him to your other half, hmm?"

"Stop it, Jules. They've met, as a matter of fact, in Dallas. We don't have that kind of thing. Nice seeing you; we have to go now. Blake's father is sick, and he wants to check on him."

Blake tried to say goodbye, but Seth jerked him away, and they drove to the hospital. Seth said, "She's always been a bitch, loving to stir up shit."

"We can talk later, but, honestly, I had wondered about Lady Pernod. You said you were boyfriends."

"I guess we are. We've been an item for a long time. We both travel, most of the time separately, and we're not stupid. He has flings, so I have mine, too."

Blake parked the car and looked at Seth, who stared straight ahead. "Is this you letting me down? I didn't plan for this. You pushed for it, but now I'm just some strange? I'm surprised that it hurts, but it does."

"I'm sorry. You're not just a fuck for me; I have strong feelings for you. I like who you are. I thought it was just a kinship with me because of our gifts. You were lonely and hurting, and I wanted to make you happy for a while."

"Wow. I think I'm actually jealous." He wanted the safety of his sadness again. He wished sex could be just a fling to him, but that wasn't in his makeup. Perhaps it was because of the lies told to him in his childhood; sex and love should be inseparable; to make them otherwise was a sin against a god he never believed existed.

It was after midnight, and the room was dark and quiet. A nurse came in and said, "He's doing better. We're sure the drugs set him off. The doctor started him on something else for the pain and something to calm him down. He said your father needs to be in a nursing home. His dementia is at a stage that takes a lot of care."

"We'll go to Phoenix, then I'll take him to Florida. My mother will decide where to put him."

The two-hundred-fifty-mile drive to the ranch had incredible scenery: desert, jagged red mountains, and valleys intricately carved from stone. Seth drove, and James lay in the back, drugged into sleep. Blake was glad he didn't have to deal with his father's dementia right now. He had withdrawn into himself, trying to understand why his chances for happiness always disappeared so quickly.

"If you can't go on to Phoenix, if your dad needs to get home, I'll understand."

"We'll see what we find out at the ranch. If it's a dead end, we might as well turn around, but I'll still take you to Phoenix. It's close. I've been considering flying Dad home from there, anyway. I'd leave my car and come back for it later. Dad can't travel alone."

"I'll take care of your car for you."

"That might work," Blake said. "We could see each other again. Whatever happens from here on out, let's not lose touch. It's my fault for expecting too much. I can't help but believe you came along for a reason."

"To make things more complicated, I'm pretty sure me and Pernod are done. It wasn't like him to take off and leave me there. Who knows? I might be single and not know it."

"That's too bad."

"Honestly, I don't care. Frankly, I don't like him screwing around on me. I go along with it because everyone does it. But being gay doesn't mean you can't be monogamous. So call me a hypocrite."

"Why do I get the feeling there's more to this story?"

"There is; I don't talk about it. Pernod's got a drug problem. I used to have one myself; it's what got me involved with him; something in common. I've been clean for five years, and I hoped he was, too, but I found him shooting up backstage in Dallas. He tried to get me to join him, but I'm not going back there. You might have saved me by coming along when I needed help."

"And you saved me from the butterflies. What are the chances?"

"Some things don't happen by chance. This could be one of them." Seth leaned over and kissed Blake on his cheek.

"But you'll see Pernod in Phoenix."

"Yes. I owe him a decent goodbye. It hasn't been *all* bad with him. I'm afraid I let him down; he needs me to keep him clean."

James groaned and raised himself from the back seat, and Blake hoped he'd be lucid for a while longer. "I've got to pee, if you don't mind."

"Sure thing, Dad. We'll stop right away."

They pulled into a gas station and Seth filled the tank while Blake helped James to the men's room. The big window in front of the building displayed souvenirs and trinkets. Seth loved the turquoise jewelry and stepped inside to have a look. He paid for the gasoline and bought a beautiful Navajo silver piece; a butterfly inlaid with turquoise and red oyster shell. It came with a handmade silver chain, and the colors would suit Blake's eyes and hair perfectly.

A Navajo man sat at a jeweler's bench in the corner, smoking a cigarette and drinking a beer. Seth asked him if he did engraving.

"Does the Pope shit in the woods?"

Seth handed him the piece and said, "How long to put some words on the back?"

"Ten minutes and ten dollars. Write here what you want on it."

Seth took the slip of paper and wrote, "May your dreams always be beautiful."

The man read it and said, "Your friend must be very special to you. My treat. Come back in ten minutes."

The men waited outside and looked at the mountains in the distance. James said, "The first time I drove this way, coming back from California, I stopped somewhere on the highway and wished I had Chief with me. I wanted to saddle him up and ride off into the landscape toward the mountains, and just forget everything else. Now I wonder if Chief saw it too, and thought of me."

Seth went inside the store and watched as the jeweler finished the engraving. His hands were brown and wrinkled from age and the sun, but Seth saw grace in them; the thousands of works of art they'd created. He picked up the piece, polished it with a cloth, and handed it to Seth. "My gift. Treasure him. I hope you don't mind that I added a prayer from me: 'May This Keep You Safe From Harm'."

CHAPTER 12

Cochise

Blake was driving, and James sat beside him in the front seat. Seth was in the back, lost in the scenery and thoughts of what lay ahead. Blake turned on the radio, and Whitney Houston was singing "Saving All My Love for You."

"You bastard, you knew that song was on!" Seth laughed and punched Blake in the shoulder.

Blake said, "No, but it's kind of appropriate."

"How long until the ranch? I hope they've got a place to eat there. I'm famished."

"We're getting close. How about some more barbecue? There was a sign a ways back; we're coming up on it now."

They entered the diner and took seats at the long stainless steel counter. James ordered the Audie Burger. "Seems like all we do is eat in restaurants. I miss my wife's cooking."

"You'll be home soon, Dad. We might be close to finding out about Chief."

"How long have we been on the road, anyway? Seems like forever, not that I can remember much of it."

"It's been a week, Dad." Blake was relieved that his father remembered anything about the trip at all, and hoped he'd stay this lucid for the rest of it. "I need to get back, too. I'm sure my work is piling up."

The woman behind the counter asked James, "How's the Audie Burger? That's one of our best sellers."

"Pretty good," James said. "You ever meet Audie?"

"No, I didn't move to Vail until after he was gone. There

are people at the ranch who knew him. They won't be around much longer, though, and that's a shame. Can I get you boys anything else?"

Blake said, "We're going there now. Any chance we can talk to those people? We're trying to find out about a horse that was there years ago. He belonged to my dad here."

The lady grinned. "Well, isn't that something? Ask for a man called Bill Watson. He worked for Audie and still takes care of the animals. He'll tell you what you want to know. But hurry; Bill's in his nineties." She laughed and picked the bill up from the counter. "This is on the house. Tell Bill that Loretta says hello."

It was an hour before they reached the ranch, driving a road that was better suited for mules. It twisted through the barren land and seemed to lead to nowhere. At last, ahead stood a few wooden buildings and a faded sign that read "AM Ranch, Welcome". Seth stopped the car in front of a building with "Office" painted over the door and went inside, but found no one there, so they drove down to a barn where a man stood outside brushing a horse.

Blake approached him and said, "Are you Bill Watson?"

"Whatever it is, I didn't do it," the man laughed. "Yep, guilty."

A few moments passed, and Blake walked back to the car and leaned in the window. "He wants to show us around a bit. Seems like a nice old guy."

"Did you ask him about Chief?" Seth said.

"Just come on. He can tell you himself."

Bill led them around the barn while telling stories of the ranch's heyday. There had been a herd of quarter horses that Audie Murphy purchased for his films, and Bill had taken care of them. Now there were only six in the stalls, and he doubted they'd be there much longer.

"But I'll never forget that beautiful palomino we had here. Nobody was allowed to ride him except Audie. He was so proud of that horse and loved to show him off to anybody who came to the ranch."

Bill paused, Blake assumed for dramatic effect, looked at James, and said slowly, "His name… was… Chief."

James sat on a bale of hay and stared at Bill, hoping he would say more. "Audie bought Chief from a friend of his in Alabama, just because Chief was so pretty. He kept him in Texas for a while, then here for around six months, then moved most of the horses to his ranch in California to make his movies there." He paused again, looked at the men, and said, "You boys thirsty? I've got some beer in the cooler."

James stared through the open barn door, out to the hills, and imagined Chief running free over them. The clear sky looked unreal, like an old Technicolor movie. He pictured Chief shining in the sunlight, his coat glistening like burnished gold. He felt the strong, smooth flanks between his legs, rode Chief toward the horizon, and took him home for the last time.

"No, we're fine. Well, what about Chief ?" Seth said, getting perturbed at the old man's reticence.

"Chief? They took him to California with the others. Audie wanted him for a movie. I don't remember which one, but I was an extra in one of them; I wanted to be a star, but they said I talked too slow."

James stood up from his hay bale and went to the barn doors, and looked at the hills. Blake wondered what he was feeling; he had to be disappointed.

"Don't go yet, mister. There's something else I want to show you. Come this way." Bill walked out of the barn and toward the corral behind it. James followed him unsteadily, helped by Seth. They reached the wooden rails of the enclosure, and Bill opened the gate, then disappeared into the shed at the far end. It seemed that a long time passed, and they felt something important was about to happen.

They heard Bill yell "Hee-yah!" and from inside the shed, a magnificent golden stallion ran into the middle of the corral, then reared high into the blue sky, his mane blowing behind him in the hot desert air. He ran toward James, stopped in front of him, and stood motionless, his big black eyes transfixed on James's face.

James gasped and clutched his chest. "Dad, are you all right?"

"That's Chief; I swear to god that's my Chief."

Bill brought a saddle, put it on the horse, and said, "Meet Cochise, Chief's grandson."

James was crying, staring at the horse, and Blake sensed he might be in trouble.

"Dad, you okay?"

"Yes, son. It's just..."

"I know, Dad, it's kind of unbelievable. I know now why you talk about Chief; how beautiful he was."

"I'm thirteen years old and Chief is alive."

Bill said, "Cochise was born after Audie died, so he never got to meet him. He was born in California, but we brought him back here to have his foal someday. It hasn't happened yet, but there's time."

Blake put his arm around his dad's shoulders and said, "This was worth the trip."

"I can die happy now, son."

Seth stood nearby, wiping away tears. Bill Watson just smiled.

"Hang on! I saddled him up for you."

Bill led Cochise out of the corral to James. He held the reins out to him and said, "Take them. I can tell he wants you to ride him."

James looked at Blake. "If you're sure you'll be okay, then do it, Dad. But let Mr. Watson lead you around a bit first until you get the feel of it. I know it's been a while. Please be careful of your leg."

Bill took Cochise into the open field and led him in circles. James sat up straight and looked confident, talked to Cochise and patted his neck. He rode to where Bill stood, leaned down from the saddle, and spoke to him. They chatted for a few moments, and Bill turned and looked at Blake, and gave the reins to James.

Blake said, "Oh, crap," and James said giddy-up and the horse began running farther out into the field. They ran from one end of the field to the other, then in circles, then toward the hurdles near the paddock.

Blake yelled, "No, Dad, no!"

He started to run toward them, but Seth grabbed his arm and said, "Let him go! Don't take this moment from him!" They held their breath as Cochise started his run toward the jump.

James was bent over the saddle horn, yelling to the horse to go faster, and in seconds, they reached the point of no return. Cochise jumped high; his enormous body seemed to become weightless, and James relaxed and let the horse lift him effortlessly into the air. He cleared the hurdle with room to spare and came to earth like an Olympian high jumper.

They drove the rough road back to Vail. James was silent and occasionally put his hands to his face to savor the lingering earthy aroma of the animal. He had hugged Cochise, rubbed his golden shoulders, kissed his forehead, and whispered, "Goodbye". He closed his eyes and relived the ride over and over; he wanted the memory to last forever.

They passed through Tucson and reached Phoenix. Seth wasn't in a hurry to get to his club, since he wouldn't be performing that night. They found the motel where his troupe was staying, and Seth said, "I don't want to stay here tonight. Can I stay with you?"

A nicer hotel was across the street, so Blake rented two adjoining rooms; one for him and Seth, and one for James, the latter having doors that locked from Blake's side. James was safe for the evening, and Seth could have one more night of privacy with Blake.

They put James to bed; he was drained from the day,

and happier than Blake had seen him in months. Blake turned out the light, and his father said, "Thank you for today, son. It was like being in heaven. I hope I remember it when I wake up."

The hotel provided a baby monitor. Blake ordered drinks from room service and a pizza from next door, and they began their night.

Later, after they'd had sex, Seth said, "Oh, I forgot something."

Blake answered, "No, I'm pretty sure you covered all the bases."

Seth laughed, got out of bed, and went to his duffel bag. Blake watched his beautiful body move across the room and wanted him again.

"Here; something to remember me by." Seth put the silver butterfly in Blake's hand. He looked at it and smiled at Seth.

"Turn it over; there's an inscription."

Blake's lower lip trembled, and Seth said, "You look like your dad when your lip does that."

"This sucks. But thank you for this. I'm going to keep it forever." He reached for Seth and kissed him, slowly and deeply.

It was dawn when Blake was awakened by the sound of James trying to open the door between the rooms. He opened it, and James stood naked in the doorway and looked confused.

"Margaret Bagley was here. She's dead, she told me. And things are flying around me, the flutterbirds."

Blake walked into the room and stopped, unable to go farther. Butterflies, lots of them, were circling in the dim light from the window. Yellow, blue, orange, and black. Moths, too; brown, striped, and huge pale ones the color of the moon.

"Seth, come here! Wake up!"

"Holy shit! Who died?"

"Margaret, Dad's old girlfriend. He said she was here and told him."

"Well, she's doing a damn good job of it."

James said, in a high-pitched whisper, "Everything she ever did is in my head. Things we did together and things we didn't. Her paintings I never saw. Her babies. Her pain. It's like I was there with her all along. They're inside my mind!"

Seth said, "It'll be okay, James. Try to relax. They'll be gone in a minute." Blake opened the window, and the insects began flying through it, out into the early morning.

James said, "I'm cold."

Blake got a bathrobe and draped it over James's shoulders. "I'm here, Dad. Don't be afraid. Think of Cochise. What a wonderful day we had."

James calmed down, looked at his son, and said, "Yeah, Chief. My horse. It was like riding him again."

"He loved you. I could tell how he looked at you."

"Like I love you, son. I'm sorry for other things, but I love you."

"I know, Dad. Let's go back to bed. The flutterbirds are going now. Get some sleep."

Blake opened the window and watched the insects fly slowly into the desert night, disappearing one by one, at first becoming translucent, then fading into the black sky.

Blake sat beside Seth on the edge of their bed, trying to make some sense of what they'd seen. "I'm going to call that nursing home in Braggville; I have to know if Margaret died. If she's dead, I'll never question this thing again."

Blake got the number from information. After many rings, a woman answered. "Are you family?"

"My father was her best friend when they were young. Please, did she pass away?"

"Just a few hours ago. We can't get hold of her kids; do you have a number?"

"No, but I wouldn't sweat it. From what I've heard, they won't care. They're not in the will."

"That's so sad. Well, tell your father I'm very sorry.

What is his name?"

"James."

"Oh, she was saying stuff about a James when she passed. She wanted to give him flowers. People say strange things when they're dying. I've seen that a lot."

"Thank you. I'll call again soon. We're traveling right now. I want to know about services and whatever. Dad would want to know."

The woman said, "As far as I know, there won't be any, unless that man who visits her wants to take care of it. How did you know to call about her?"

"Just a hunch. Thanks again."

"Are you the fella that was visiting here the other day? With two other men?"

"Yes, I was there."

"I'm the nurse who was on duty in the TV room. We both saw it. I winked at you, but I wasn't flirting. They're here all the time before someone dies. Be careful. It can make you crazy," then the line went silent.

Blake put the phone down and said, "Okay, smart ass, I don't know how you knew someone died, but I believe you now. I believe all of it. My butterflies, his butterflies, Margaret's butterflies. I mean, why the fuck is it butterflies?"

"Don't forget the moths. They're about the darker things."

"Help me. I'm trying to make sense of this."

"Okay, I'll try to explain. Margaret loved James, but they couldn't be together, right?"

"Yes. They wanted to, but their lives just never meshed."

"Margaret lived her life without the man she loved, and she wanted him to know everything about it, all the things he missed, so it would be like they'd lived them together. It was her gift to him. After all, they'd never get the chance to talk about all the things they'd been through. It's sad."

Something connected in Blake's mind, like when a child grasps the concept of multiplication tables.

"And it's happening to me with Dad because he's dying, but one piece at a time?"

"Yes, and not just with your dad. Remember the tornado? But it's all okay; it's natural and beautiful, so don't be afraid. Your father wants you to know things about him he could never tell you, but they're still his truth; his history. Some people believe that if your story goes on without you, you never die. And he loves you; he wants you to know who he is, all of it, the good and the bad."

"But the butterflies, they look so real."

"Don't worry. Only the people they're carrying memories for, and people like us, can see them. So don't go waving your arms around to shoo them away. You might end up next to your dad in the home."

Blake decided to stay another night in Phoenix; he wanted to see Seth perform and say hello to Pernod. He was trying to be more open-minded and hoped it might help to see Seth with his boyfriend, if that's what he still was.

He called the hotel desk and asked for a florist, then ordered a dozen white roses to be delivered to Seth backstage, knowing that Pernod would ask who sent them.

James dressed in his best jeans and jacket, and Blake put on the butterfly necklace. They took a cab to the bar; Blake didn't want to risk getting lost on the way back. After dinner in the club's restaurant, they sat in the showroom as the show was beginning. It was mediocre until Madame Psyche took the stage.

She was stunning, beautiful, and made the other queens look like amateurs. Madame Psyche did Judy, Billie, and Whitney, with three costume changes. Her act moved the crowd to put lots of high-denomination bills into her eager, jeweled hands.

She left the stage for a moment, then returned for another bow, carrying a bouquet. Blake was crestfallen that it wasn't white roses. Seth waved to him in the audience, then looked at James, threw him a kiss, held up the flowers, and mouthed "For you". Blake had seen flowers like them before, on a faded sign on a plate glass window that read "Wild Iris Cafe."

Men in and out of dresses packed the dressing room. Feathers, shed from boas tossed onto mirrors, floated in the air, and glitter coated the wooden floor. The sound of champagne corks popping and screams of laughter had turned the night into a party. Seth sat at his dressing table wiping makeup from his face. He looked up at Blake and said, "I haven't thanked you for the roses," and waved his hand toward the bouquet next to him. "But these irises are special. I thought there'd been a mistake, or James sent them, but when I read the card a second time, I realized they're not for me, but for him. Even has his last name on it. I asked the delivery boy, and he said some lady called in the order and said to deliver them to me. It's like she knew he'd be here."

Seth winked at Blake and handed the bouquet to James, who looked at them and smiled.

"Margaret," James whispered.

Blake said, "So, where's Pernod? Did she perform? Everyone was so made up I couldn't tell if she was one of the girls."

"They wouldn't let her on stage. She was too high. She's in the back now, probably shooting up again," Seth answered. "Your roses set her off. I guess she needs me more than I realized. She's so afraid I'll leave her, but she puts on an act like she doesn't care."

"Sorry about the roses. Why can't you just..." Blake tried to finish, but Seth raised his hand and shook his head.

"I've been where he is. I can't leave him like that; I'm just not that cruel."

"I don't want you to go. I've never said that to anyone before, but I don't want you to go."

"Why not? You just need me to protect you from your butterflies. I can't do that forever. I do have feelings for you, but if I don't try to help Pernod, at least give it one more shot,

I'll never forgive myself."

"So, just like that, you're going back to him, drugs and all?"

"That's *why* I'm going back, the drugs, and all."

"We haven't known each other very long, but dammit, you made me feel like maybe I could have someone in my life again. I haven't wanted that in a long, long time."

"That's great, Blake. Don't stop."

"I want to have some more time with you to find out if this means something."

"It does mean something. But I need to be with Pernod right now, for me, too."

"So, the sex, and all the sweet talk, and you pulling me out of the dark; that was just... what?

"The sex was because I like you, and we both needed someone. It may become something else, but I have to get rid of my baggage first, or we won't work out."

"Well, go and get rid of your baggage, then. And thanks for fucking me up even more."

"That's not fair."

"You made this happen, Seth. I need you now. Please."

"If this is meant to be, it will. Trust me on that. I have faith we'll find each other if we still feel this way."

"Goddammit, then go. Maybe catch you later. Thanks for your help, and I do mean that. You got me through some shit. But this sucks."

Seth took a card from his wallet. "Look, this is the number of the salon where I work in St. Louis. I keep in touch with them; they'll always know where I am. Please call them if you need to. I hope you will."

Blake took the card, and without looking at it said, "Thanks, but I won't use this anytime soon; I want you to have some time to decide what you want. I mean it. I hope we get together again. It feels like there was a reason we met like this."

Blake looked at his father and said, "Well, Dad, I guess it's me and you now."

Seth hugged James and said, "Go find your horse. He's out there. You take care of Blake; I'll be thinking about you two." James looked around the room, then at Blake, and his eyes were full of questions; Blake feared that confusion was overtaking him.

"Come on, Dad, let's get you into bed."

James reached for Seth's hand and said, "I hope I can remember you. You're a good man."

Seth said, "I'll send you a flutterbird. You won't forget."

That night, Blake lay in his hotel bed, stared at the bouquet of irises on the dresser, said, "Motherfucker," and felt a space opening inside him again that he hadn't realized had been filled, and even fighting the feeling didn't make it go away. He wouldn't let himself cry or be hurt, so he settled for anger. A long night lay ahead of him.

CHAPTER 13
Tired and Confused

Seth took his bags downstairs and phoned for a taxi. Blake offered to drive him, but he preferred to go alone. Pernod might be stoned, angry, or otherwise fucked-up.

It had cooled to a bearable temperature outside. The heat in Phoenix was insufferable until the sun set and the cool wind from the faraway mountains blew across the desert. He reached the nightclub, and the driver helped him carry his things backstage.

Pernod was in the dressing room, applying her makeup. "Well, look what the cat dragged in. I wondered if you'd make it."

"I have a show to do. And I need the money. Are you up to performing ?"

"Sorry about last night. I kind of lost it. I was glad to see you; it's been strange without you. The show needs you, too. You are the star, after all."

Mark looked at the clock on the dressing table. "So, sweetie, you *are* working tonight, I hope. You're on stage in one hour."

"Oh, damn! I haven't dressed."

"Here, baby, let me help you with that. You look tired. Your usual face tonight?"

"Sure, it worked last night."

Pernod began transforming Seth into Madam Psyche, a process that was magical to see. In an hour, she became a gorgeous, vivacious, foul-mouthed star, and a comedienne with a beautiful singing voice. She mimicked the greatest entertainers in the world, dead and alive, and could bring her audience to tears if she wished; that was her favorite thing to do.

She gave her best performance and sang love songs, and all the time thought of Blake.

Afterward, undressing next to Mark, Seth said, "I'll stay with the group. Isn't LA next?"

"Yep, then it's all over unless you head north. They're booking a gig in Portland, and maybe Seattle."

"I might do that. I've never been up that way, and I could use the money. I want to stay out of the salon as long as possible. And St. Louis isn't doing it for me anymore."

"You'll find something in Seattle," Mark said. "So, what do we do now? What am I to you? Are you here for the work, or am I part of the attraction?"

"You're the one who took off. You don't get to cop an attitude. We both did what we had to do. A lot depends on you; I can't be around your drugs again. You're sickening when you're stoned. You know what I've been through; I won't go back there."

"I'm trying. I can't promise, but I *am* trying."

The hotel was a step above seedy. Mark asked Seth to stay in his room because they had things to discuss, but it was three in the morning and Seth was too exhausted to talk. He slipped into bed, and Mark joined him and pulled his body closer to him. His hand moved to Seth's stomach; he pushed it away.

"So, that's the way it is?"

"I'm tired and confused. I need space right now."

"It's that guy, isn't it? What was his name?"

"His name is Blake, and yeah, we had a thing, but he's gone now. I'm sure you haven't been crowned Miss Celibate."

"I assumed you might want us to be the way we were."

"No, Mark, I would never want that, not with the crazy

shit. I'm here because I worry about you. And the show is my job, remember?"

"I see. But worry about me? I'm fine. And I want you back."

"I doubt it's a great idea, but we'll see. I'm afraid of the junk, and I refuse to ever get hit again."

"I was out of my mind stoned."

"Yes, that's my point."

The troupe did seven shows in Phoenix, then went to LA to begin their run. Mark was on his best behavior, but Seth knew his motive was to show he had the strength to quit using drugs. The club was fabulous, and the LA crowd loved Madam Psyche. Seth was elated that the jaded Hollywood boys gave him such a wonderful reception.

Mark, however, showed his envy. Seth hated that Mark usually became a vicious, jealous queen if his applause or the tips weren't as good as Seth's. When he got in that mood, the needle would come out, and he'd disappear, sometimes for days.

It was the last night of their run in LA. The house was packed. All the performers worked their hardest, but Madam Psyche slayed them. After a raucous performance of music and mind reading, she closed her act with "I'll Be Seeing You", a slow, soft, nostalgic song about missing someone you loved who went away, and imagining them in the places they used to go. The audience thought she sang to them, but it was to someone else altogether.

The dressing room was filled with visitors, and the girls entertained them with giggles and champagne. Seth looked around but didn't see Pernod. The manager came in, hugged and kissed everyone, and announced that the troupe was going to Portland for a two-week run, and then to Seattle. He glanced at Seth, who nodded and mouthed, "Count me in."

The tour bus would leave early the next morning, so Seth worked his way through the crowd to the street, signing autographs and kissing strangers on his way to a waiting taxi.

The hotel room was in disarray. He began to finish packing. A high-pitched voice came from the bathroom; the door was ajar, and a light was on. The voice wasn't Mark's, but then he heard Mark laugh. He looked through the crack in the door. Mark sat on the closed commode, a needle and rubber tourniquet on the floor beside him, and a spoon and cigarette lighter in the sink. Between his thighs bobbed the blonde-wigged head of one of the drag queens: Marilyn Monroe, still in her high heels. Seth hardly knew her but despised her all the same.

Mark's head rested on the toilet tank; he turned to Seth; his eyes were red slits. "Hi, Seth, baby. Want some stuff?"

Mark pushed the man off of him, and Seth pulled Marilyn up by her bustier and said, "Get out of here, now!" She grabbed her dress and fled to the bedroom, and in a moment slammed the room door shut.

"Fuck you, Miss Star. Why'd you do that? Jealous much?"

"No. Disgusted."

"Like I said, fuck you. I'm sick of your holier-than-thou shit. Why don't you get the fuck out of my life?"

"At last, we agree on something. I can't help you anymore. I came back here because I used to care about you. There was a time when I wanted to be with you and thought we might be good together. Not anymore. Now I know it was just the dope. If you want to die, go ahead; I'm going to live. Have fun."

"You'll be sorry if you leave me."

Seth laughed. "Leaving you will be a huge relief; you're a loser." Mark stood up, hung onto the sink, and tried to grab Seth's arm.

"You're too fucked up to hit me. That's so pitiful, but it's making this easy."

"I won't be like this tomorrow. You'd better watch your back, and your boyfriend's, too. I'd like to kill you both."

"Good luck with that; I don't even know where he is."

Sleeping on the bus wasn't too bad; he wasn't tall, and the seats were spacious. In any case, it was better than staying in the hotel room with Mark. He had a few hours before the bus would leave, so he made himself comfortable and closed his eyes.

The driver was asleep in the bus shed, but woke at dawn and brought Seth coffee and a Danish. An hour later, the seats filled with drag queens and the stage crew. After a head count, the bus swayed and rolled out of the station. Seth looked out to the street. A sloppily dressed drag queen, holding a wilted white rose, stood on the curb, but the driver didn't stop for her; she looked more like a disheveled homeless woman than a performer.

Someone in the next row said, "Thank god they finally got rid of her ass." As they passed Mark, he staggered to the curb and held an object in the air, lifted his other hand, and followed the bus as he shot a bird at the occupants.

Seth looked at him and laughed at the obscene gesture, then saw the object he held high: a shiny, black handgun.

CHAPTER 14

Put the Tip In It

"Mother, it's only five hours to Los Angeles. We might as well go the whole way; we've come so far already." Blake sat on the bed in the hotel room with the phone in one hand and a map in the other. He had packed their bags and was ready to leave for California. His mother was not happy, and he was trying to calm her down.

"He's doing fine. He's healing well from the accident and seems to be having a great time. After we go to the ranch in LA, we'll get on a plane to Florida."

There was silence on the phone line as Mary pictured her husband flying across a continent.

"I'll come and get him," she said. "You'd have to leave your car somewhere and then fly back for it. That doesn't make sense."

"Let me think about that. If it gets to be too much, I'll call you. I want him to finish this trip with me."

They began the drive toward Los Angeles. Blake wished he could detour to the Grand Canyon, but James seemed to be showing the strain of the trip, and had been out of sorts most of the time; short-tempered and confused more often about where they were, and frequently didn't recognize him. Perhaps it was time to send him home.

They reached Palm Springs after driving for hours through the beige desert landscape, the air outside the car so hot that cracking a window was like lighting a blow torch.

James was exhausted and hungry; Blake decided they'd spend the night in Palm Springs.

He found a motel just outside the city limits. The building was a 1950s classic, but it didn't offend Blake's sensibilities. Perhaps, he thought, a queer architect had designed it. The lines were very refined for the period, not attempting to replicate moon rockets or spinning atoms.

At dinner, they sat outside by the pool next to the restaurant. The air had become cool, and the sky was clear and sparkled with stars. It looked like the sky over the Gulf of Mexico, and Blake wondered if James could remember that.

A handsome young waiter approached them and asked if they'd like a cocktail. Blake said yes, and James nodded his head, and soon they were sipping daiquiris and enjoying the breeze from the desert.

"Dad, tomorrow we'll go to the town where Audie Murphy sent Chief to be in the movies. I hope we can find out more about him that way. But don't be disappointed if we can't; it's been a long time."

"I know, son. But don't worry; seeing Chief's grandson was almost as good as seeing him."

The waiter had been watching them through the restaurant window, and Blake motioned for him to bring the check. "You can put your room number on it and sign it if you'd rather," he said.

Blake smiled up at him, aware of his bright green eyes and soft smile. "Which way is best for you?"

"Oh, signing it is easiest for me. If you want, you can put the tip in it."

Blake looked up at the man and grinned.

"*On* it." He paused while Blake wrote. "It looks like he's ready for some sleep," he said, glancing at James, who was leaning sideways in the chair and snoring. "I work until eleven."

"Thanks, but I need to stay with my dad. He has nightmares and dementia."

"Oh well, thanks for the tip."

"I might pass through here on my way home without my dad."

The man smiled and said, "Be sure to stop and say hello. I have a room here." He wrote something on a blank guest check and handed it to Blake. "That's my phone and room number," then winked and walked away.

James sat up, wiped the spit from the corner of his mouth, and said, "You ought to take him up on his offer. I'll be fine."

"You heard all that?"

"Go in there and tell him you'll meet up with him later. You don't have to take all night, for god's sake! Do I have to teach you everything?"

Blake took the bill inside, chatted with the server, arranged to meet, and borrowed a baby monitor from the front desk.

The guy was gorgeous naked; he had a smooth, muscular body and was fun to be with, but he thought of Seth and their times in bed. They still meant something to him. He tried to put aside his ingrained guilt and the feeling that he was being unfaithful to someone who had never asked for his fidelity or love. As the beautiful young man finished and kissed his chest, Blake whispered, "See what I did? Fuck you, Seth."

It took an hour to reach the Audie Murphy Ranch. Halfway through the drive, James's face became pale and contorted, as if he was fighting tears, and afraid. He leaned forward, clutched the dashboard, and said, "I don't know where I am. Where are you taking me? Are you going to hurt me?"

"No, Dad, of course not. We're going to the place where your horse en

ded up, the one you had when you were a boy."

"You're a lying motherfucker. I never had a horse, and I don't know who the hell you are. Take me home. My leg hurts. You hit me, didn't you?"

Blake stopped the car on the shoulder of the road. He sat, silent, and stared ahead at the dry landscape. The only structure was a little shack up ahead with a sign that read "Strawberries for Sale". His heart pounded, and for the first time, he feared his father. The tone of James's voice had become vicious and threatening. The hair on Blake's arms stood.

He offered James the water bottle that he kept between them. James's hand shook as he took it and looked Blake in the eyes, squinting, his head tilted to one side.

"Was there a horse? I touched him?"

"Yes, Dad, we did. Remember? You saw Chief 's grandson. Now we're going to see where Chief lived after you had him."

James looked down at the floorboard and shook his head. "I can't remember all of that. Not right now, but it will come to me."

"We'll see where he lived, then go home, okay, Dad?"

"I hope it's soon. I don't feel well. What's happening to me? Please don't hurt me anymore."

Blake's eyes stung from the tears forming in them. He wiped his eyes on his sleeve and tried to stop their flow, but still, they came, hot and burning. His father leaned toward him, gently pushed Blake forward, and began patting his back.

"It's okay. Don't cry. We'll find our way home."

Shortly before reaching the ranch, James said, "I have to pee, right now." Blake stopped at a gas station, helped his father into the men's room, and left him there while he filled the car. He kept an eye on the restroom door. The gas tank was almost empty and took a long time to fill, and James still hadn't emerged from the toilet. Blake paid the attendant, then sprinted to the door. It was locked. Blake knocked softly first, then harder, and called out, "Dad!" There was no response. The attendant came running; he'd heard Blake's voice and the urgency and fear in it. The man fumbled with the keys hanging from his belt and unlocked the door.

James was on the toilet with his pants around his ankles and a frown on his face.

He looked at the men and said, "There's no damn toilet paper in here, and it stinks like something died."

Blake apologized to the attendant, who fake-smiled and said, "I'll get some."

Blake stopped at the first motel he saw and rented a room for the night. It was lunchtime, and James was hungry, so Blake brought food from the motel cafe. He wasn't comfortable taking his father out in public after his mood of the morning. They ate burgers and fries, and James talked about his past.

"You know, I had a horse once. He was a beauty. I was a kid. I can't remember his name, though."

"His name was Chief," Blake said. His father's eyes seemed focused on something far away, as if he could see through the aging wallpapered walls of the motel room. The window air conditioner hummed and rattled, and the sound of children screaming with joy in the swimming pool outside attacked Blake's ears.

"I had a horse, but I don't remember his name. That was a long time ago, I think."

"Yes, Dad, a long time ago."

James guided a French fry toward his mouth, and Blake was relieved when it reached its destination. James closed his eyes as he chewed. "Mmm, that's good," he said, smiled, then looked at Blake and said, "You're a good cook, like your mother. Where is she, anyway?"

"She's at home, taking care of things until we get back. I'll call her later, and you can talk to her."

"You lie to me a lot. You know she's dead. I saw the flyers."

"Okay, Dad. Just eat and don't worry about anything. Mother is fine, you'll see."

James finished the last bite of his hamburger, leaned

back in his chair, closed his eyes, and said, "So, you want to hear about my horse?"

James slept while Blake phoned his mother; he knew it was time for her to come.

Morning came, and Blake sat on the edge of the tub while his dad showered. James had trouble using the shampoo but was able to rinse his hair on his own. He seemed to love feeling the water on his skin. Blake looked at his father's naked body and remembered how muscular it used to be. His skin was pale and wrinkled, as if time had etched itself into it as rivers do to canyons, then sprinkled it with brown paint from a talentless artist's brush.

His once well-shaped, taut legs and buttocks were now thin and dissolving into uselessness, and Blake knew his future was looking back at him. The thought terrified him. Almost everyone on his father's side of the family had died with dementia, or Alzheimer's, and Blake expected he would, too.

He'd decided that if the time came, he'd end it all, and had researched painless ways to kill himself; death was better than forgetting your whole life, or who you were. He didn't want someone cleaning his ass for him, or feeding him, or talking to him like the idiot he would become.

James said, almost inaudibly above the flow of water, "I used to live by a river, and I had a horse." Then, he began to sing, "Let me call you sweetheart…"

CHAPTER 15
The Movie

The next morning, while James was still asleep, Blake made plane reservations for his mother; she would arrive in Los Angeles in two days.

They stopped for lunch, then drove onto the ranch property and found miles of cheaply built but high-priced houses where the fields had been.

"We're not gonna find many horses here, Blake."

"Doesn't look that way, does it? Sorry, Dad. But it was Audie Murphy's Ranch. I guess it's ruined like every place else. Maybe we can find something about the ranch and where they kept the horses. It could be someone will remember Chief."

They drove onto a street with fast food restaurants and boutiques, and Blake looked down the street and saw the marquee of a theater, older than the surrounding buildings. Blake loved the Art Deco architecture and the colorful old movie posters near the ticket window with pictures of horses and cowboys in them. The big sign on the canopy had lighted letters that blinked the word Mariposa, one letter at a time. Under that, the removable letters on the marquee spelled "Audie Murphy Retrospective".

Blake said, "Care to catch a movie?"

His father said, "Why? I want to see a horse."

"There'll be lots of them in the movie, I'm sure."

"Well, I have to pee. Might as well go in there to do it."

They went into the theater, and James's attention was caught by one of the posters. He touched the glass near the illustration of a blonde horse in the distance. A baby-faced cowboy rode a dark stallion in the foreground. "That's a palomino," he said.

"Come on, Dad, let's go inside."

Blake helped James use the men's room and then led him into the theater. The air conditioning made them feel as if they had dived into frigid water, and James said, "This place is colder than Makissa Springs."

Blake said, "We were there when I was a kid. I remember it was so clear and pretty. It's near where you were born."

"What was?"

"The springs you used to swim in a long time ago."

"Oh, I don't recall."

The room darkened as the first feature began. The title, in 1950s three-dimensional lettering, swiped its way across the screen: "Storm in the Desert". From far away, moving toward the camera, came a horse and rider, running full gallop, until they stopped and filled most of the frame. The horse reared itself high against the cloudless sky and jagged mountain peaks, and the wind blew the horse's long mane to one side. Raising his hat into the air in the classic rodeo pose, the rider waved it in circles as the horse came down. The animal's size was impressive, and the man on him was too diminutive for a cowboy hero. His baby face made him appear very young, but neither Blake nor his dad was focused on him.

The horse was big and regal and looked into the camera lens as if on cue. He was Technicolor blond and shone like gold in the sun. It was a breathtaking sight; James gasped and turned to look at Blake and grabbed his hand on the seat armrest, squeezed it hard, and turned back to the screen. Blake nodded.

James said, "That's Chief. I know it. Goddammit, we found him." He got up from his seat, moved slowly into the aisle, and began walking to the front. Blake followed him to the empty seats in the first row and they sat, leaning backward, and watched the horse run through the desert. Audie roped wayward steers, shot a bad man, visited his Indian friends, and finally loped into a dust-covered movie village of wooden buildings.

The rider dismounted, tied his horse to a railing, and sauntered into a saloon, where a blonde woman dressed in red satin and ruffles welcomed him and poured a shot of whiskey. She smiled as she handed it to him across the bar. Audie Murphy said, "You know I don't drink that stuff. Give me a sarsaparilla, honey."

The woman laughed and leaned over the bar and kissed the man, saying, "Good to have you back."

Neither James nor Blake were interested in the story; they wanted to see Chief again. Soon enough, the scene switched to Audie riding his horse through the desert until he reached a big, old wooden house in the empty landscape. A screen door swung open and banged against the wall as a child ran from inside, and up to the horse, who nodded toward her, nuzzled her blond hair, and pawed the dry earth. Audie got down from the horse, and a woman rushed toward him from the big front porch and collided with him in a passionate hug and kiss.

"Lance," she whispered to him, "You've come back."

"Of course I have. I told you I would."

The three of them walked onto the porch, and soon were drinking lemonade and talking of the time they'd been apart.

"Chief looks as beautiful as ever," the woman said. "Annie, go get the feed bag. He looks hungry." Audie pumped water into the trough while the little girl ran into the field toward a barn, its red paint faded to pale orange and its roof in need of repairs. The sky gradually grew dark with clouds, and Annie returned with the bag of feed. Audie picked her up and helped her tie it around Chief's neck.

She ran inside the house and returned with a net on the end of a short wooden pole, held it toward Audie, and said, "Mama made it for me, for catching butterflies. I need some for school. We're studying bugs. Mama, can I go catch some? There are real pretty ones by the barn."

"Okay, honey, but only for a few minutes. It looks like rain coming."

Blake whispered to James, "Dad, are you believing this? She's going to catch butterflies? I think Audie heard that story when he was in Texas."

James said, "So what," shrugged, and turned back to the screen.

"You don't remember Helen and the ranch and her story about the little girl in the tornado?"

"When was that?"

"Never mind, Dad. I'll tell you later."

The movie couple was oblivious to the approaching rain as they sat in the swing and held hands, gazing into each other's eyes. The camera shots switched from close-ups of their faces and entwined fingers to views of the field and the girl now far away, and the gray, roiling sky above her.

A black finger of whirling clouds descended to earth and sucked the dry soil into it, spinning faster and faster. A closeup showed the little girl's face frozen in horror, followed by a shot of the adults still on the porch, but standing now and screaming at the girl to come back to the house. Chief jumped and pulled his reins from the post. The tornado grew immense and moved in the direction of the girl, now too frightened to move. Audie ran to Chief, untied him, and jumped into the saddle. Chief ran at full gallop toward the girl, and the film sped up so it looked as if Chief was almost flying toward her.

The tornado appeared to be only yards away from Annie as Chief approached her, and Audie reached down, grabbed her by her shoulders, and lifted her into the saddle with him. Annie grasped the horn, and her blonde hair flew behind her in a visual echo of Chief's mane. Behind them, the twister roared and turned, and for a moment looked as if it would obliterate them. They disappeared into the dust and darkness; Annie began crying, "Mama!". Chief's hooves pounding the ground were louder in the soundtrack than the tornado's roar.

Audie held Annie around her waist, but she lost her grip on the saddle horn and flew up into the wind. Chief jumped high into the whirling dust as if he were clearing a hurdle, and the moment Annie was torn from Audie's hands, Chief, in mid-jump, grabbed the girl's dress in his teeth and pulled her down toward him. Audie reached for her and brought her back down to the saddle, and just as it seemed impossible for them to be saved, the storm dwindled and lifted back into the clouds.

Annie had stopped crying, and her arms were around Chief's neck. Her mother ran to them, screaming Annie's name. She fell into her mother's arms and cried into her hair.

In the next scene, the sky was clear and Annie sat in her mother's lap with Audie beside them in the swing. The woman smiled. "How can I ever thank you enough?"

"Well," Audie answered, "It's Chief you should thank. He's the hero. But if you *really* want to thank me..." He paused, and the lady frowned, narrowed her eyes, and looked at him. Audie said, "Marry me!"

Annie jumped into her mother's lap and squealed, "Momma, say yes, say yes!"

The woman looked at Chief and said, "What do you think, Chief?"

The horse ran a few feet away from them, reared again, and whinnied, obviously happy. A shot of Annie kissing Audie on the cheek ended with her saying, "I lost my butterfly net!"

The mother answered, "But you caught a daddy!"

There was laughter, and a full frame of Chief jumping toward the sky, and the ending credits crawled upward. The last one read "and Audie Murphy's Favorite Steed, Chief, the Real Star of Our Show."

Blake turned to James, who was smiling but had tears in his eyes. "So, Dad, I guess we know now. Chief became a genuine movie star."

"He sure was a magnificent horse. Reminds me of one I had when I was a kid."

"That was him, Dad, that was Chief in the movie."

"Well, I'll be damned."

CHAPTER 16
Please Call an Ambulance

Blake saw the wings flutter from his father's forehead, and from around his ears, and some came from his chest. They flew toward him and he instinctively brushed them away, but the butterflies were not afraid of his hands. There were yellow ones, blue ones, one even a bright scarlet, like no butterfly Blake had ever seen. Then came some dark, small-winged insects; moths in different shades of brown and black.

He looked at his arms and his chest, his fingers and palms, and the insects were lighting there, caressing his skin with their legs as if they were feeling him; uncoiling the long tubular organs from their heads and tasting him. He sat still and let them stay, watching them in the dim light from the screen, now showing a classic cartoon. The soundtrack was incongruous and hideously out of place. Elmer Fudd was speaking as a huge violet butterfly landed squarely on Blake's nose and tickled his nostrils.

Blake felt he would be sick; the nausea rose in his throat and he wanted to get out of the theater, away from these creatures, and his father. But the visions began, and he could not move. The sound of the film became inaudible. He looked at the screen and saw a montage of his father's life, in full color, with beautiful shots of Florida, women, California redwood trees, and a night in a cafe in a little town in Louisi-ana. People were singing, and he felt James's love for the pretty woman that embraced him. Then, his very young mother filled a paper bag with candy.

A brown moth buzzed on Blake's ear; he felt its tiny wings and feet on him. A scene appeared on the screen of a man running in a dark field, screaming in pain. There was a hand holding a long piece of metal or wood that came crashing into the young man's skull, and blood covered Blake's eyes. The screams stopped, and the moth flew toward the dark ceiling of the theater.

He thought of Seth and heard his sweet voice saying, "Only the people they're carrying memories for, and people like us with the gift, can see them." He wished Seth were there with him now, and was not surprised to feel a quick pang of sadness and longing in his gut.

The butterflies disappeared, but soon there was a small white one in front of him, then another. The two seemed to be together. On the movie screen appeared two women, early in their adulthood, embracing. They kissed. James opened a door and saw the women standing in near darkness by an unmade bed. They looked angry and panicked and told James to leave them alone. Blake thought something about one of the women's haughty voice seemed familiar. He caught the aroma of flowers and tried to remember where he'd encountered the scent before. The movie ended, and the screen went dark. A young man was shaking his shoulder, saying, "Mister, the movie's over. Is your friend there all right? He doesn't look too good."

Blake looked at his father. He was slumped to one side, and his mouth was open with spittle hanging from it. Blake shook him, and James looked up, raised his hand a couple of inches, pointed toward the movie screen, and said, so softly that Blake leaned over to hear him, "Chief. My Chief," then smiled at Blake and closed his eyes.

Blake looked up at the uniformed usher who had awakened him and said, "Please call nine-one-one."

James stopped breathing twice in the ambulance as it screamed its way to the hospital. Workers in green rushed him inside and took him into the depths of the building. Blake found a pay phone hanging in a hallway and called his mother to tell her what had happened. She seemed calm, considering her husband might be dying, but she'd always been that way in an emergency. He never understood how she could be so cool during a disaster. "I'll be there tomorrow morning, but you know that," she said. "Can you still pick us up at the airport?"

"Yes, Mother, but who is *us*?"

"Evelyn's coming with me. We thought it'd be a good idea if I had someone to help me with Dad on the trip home."

"I wish you had let me in on this sooner so I could've prepared myself. And I wish you hadn't agreed to this. I could have gone back with you; we discussed that."

"I didn't want to put you through all that. This will be fine. Evelyn's not as bad as she used to be; you'll see."

A doctor found Blake as he walked to the waiting room. Standing in the hallway, the man, older, white-coated, olive-skinned, and expressionless, said, "He's out of danger right now, but he had a terrible stroke. We can't tell if he will recover from it. He's comfortable now and sleeping. You can see him if you want to."

Blake looked into the half-open door of his father's room. James's eyes were closed, his chest rising and falling from the air forced into his lungs, the rhythm of the machine reminding Blake of the oil wells on the highway. He touched his father's hand, but James stayed still with no reaction except an almost imperceptible movement of his eyelids.

Blake tried to ignore the insects appearing from under the sheet that covered James's body as if they passed through the fabric like birds through white summer clouds. He didn't want to deal with any more of that. He had enough memories to process for today, so, as Seth said he could, he willed them to disappear. They rose to the ceiling and faded into the harsh fluorescent light.

Los Angeles International was choked with cars. Blake parked at Arrivals and waited until his mother and Evelyn, carrying makeup cases and dressed to the nines, came through the big glass doors. Two skycaps wheeled their luggage toward the curb, and Blake blew the horn and waved, and got out to open the trunk and stow their bags. His mother hugged him, and Blake tried not to withdraw from Evelyn's advance as she came toward him and held out her case like a queen expecting service from an underling. Blake said nothing. He opened the front passenger door for his mother first, then the back seat door for Evelyn.

A sweet smell replaced the odor of jet fuel as he helped her navigate the low car door opening. His aunt's scent assaulted him. His thoughts froze for a moment; his brain attempted to connect the memories, then one jumped to the front of his mind: the odor of the flowers in his vision yesterday, of two women embracing, and he realized at that moment that it was not flowers, but Evelyn's outdated perfume.

Blake whispered to himself, "Well, I'll be goddamned."

They drove to the hospital and hardly spoke except to remark about the heavy traffic and heat, and the brown pollution that obscured the distant mountain views.

Mary spoke to Evelyn. "I remember when you came out here years ago. Too bad you didn't get that movie part."

Evelyn shook her head at Mary and glanced at Blake, who was trying to picture what he'd just heard. "It was for the best. I don't think the Hollywood life would have been what Jesus wanted for me. He looks out for his sheep."

Blake glanced at his mother, who bowed her head and rubbed her temples, covering her expression with her palms. Blake knew she was trying not to laugh out loud; he was dying to utter a bleat.

At James's room, Blake suggested that he and Evelyn wait outside so his mother could have some private time with her husband. Blake tried to start a conversation with his aunt in the empty waiting room. At first, she seemed perturbed, but Blake wanted to goad her into having to speak to him.

"You've worn that perfume for a long time, haven't

you? I remember it when I was little. It used to make me sneeze."

"I guess you've outgrown that," she answered. "It's hard to find nowadays, but I still like it." She was looking through a magazine and ignoring Blake's stare.

"The scent of it must bring back a lot of memories for you."

She looked at him, her expression softened, and her eyes shifted toward the window and the dirty brown sky outside. "Yes, it does."

"Aunt Evelyn, I've spent some time alone now with my dad, you know. On the road, in motels, sitting by the Gulf. I've heard that people in his condition tend to talk out of school a lot. Dad's been telling me stories from when he was younger; he remembers those things better than what happened yesterday. And some things he's not supposed to tell just come out anyway. The filter is gone."

Evelyn's face had gone pale, and her red lipstick glowed against her translucent white skin like a cardinal in a field of snow.

"I've heard that to be true." She said, her voice taking on a defensive tone, and stared at him, trying to read his expression.

"He told me one about you."

"I can't imagine what that might be. Anyway, people with dementia imagine things. You must have learned that by now."

"No, everything he's told me I know to be true; they actually happened."

"How could you? How can you believe a person with dementia can be trusted to tell the truth?"

Despite how she'd always treated him, Blake felt sorry for his aunt, knowing her pain so well. "Aunt Evelyn, I've been where you are. Trust me, it's better on the other side."

"I don't need you to give me advice; I have Jesus for that. I found Him, and my life changed. He wants me to stay this way."

"I'll never tell a soul, at least until I get Dad's problem, perhaps. And you'll probably be dead by then, and your whole life will have passed by as a lie."

"I still don't know what you're talking about." Evelyn stood at the window and imagined she saw the Hollywood sign far away through the brown Los Angeles haze.

"Aunt Evelyn, if there's anyone in this family who understands what you're going through, it's me. Why won't you let yourself be happy?"

Evelyn wept. She reached into her purse and brought a flower-embroidered handkerchief up to her face. She would not turn around and let Blake see her cry.

She said, "I'm sorry I've treated you the way I have. You're a good man."

"Sometimes we hate in others the things that we hate most in ourselves."

"Your dad said that to me once."

"Yes, he did."

Blake smiled at Evelyn, and she began to talk again. "I came out here to audition for a movie. I was so young. It was a stupid dream of a naive girl. After what happened..." She paused and took a deep breath, "I needed to get out of my little town before anyone else found out. I would have been ruined. Your dad liked me then and promised it would remain a secret between us until the day he died. I trusted him. He kept that secret until now. I guess he's dying, so he did keep his word."

"So, he walked in on you?"

She faced Blake, and her words came faster, pouring out from a secret place that had been locked and buried for a long, dark time. "Yes, with a lady from my church. She was married. Neither of us understood what was happening, but we got swept up in it; we'd never known passion before."

"You were a beauty. I've seen the pictures. I can under-stand how anyone would be attracted to you."

"Those were headshots I had made to take with me on my big, stupid adventure. They were making a movie, and

Audie Murphy was the star. I had a crush on him; go figure. They told me he saw my photo in a pile of other young hopefuls and said I wasn't his type. A man came out of his office and said, 'You can go now, Mr. Murphy has found his lady.' "

"Dad and I were watching an old Audie Murphy film when he had his stroke," Blake said, looking up at Evelyn, who was still drying her tears. "It had Dad's horse in it. There was a tornado."

Evelyn's handkerchief dropped to the floor. She sat down and looked at Blake. "Your dad's horse? Chief? I had no idea. But the tornado... that was the movie I tried out for."

She reached to retrieve her fallen handkerchief. "Blake, since we seem to be talking now, there's something I'd like to ask you. I've always wondered, you being out and everything, why you never had a boyfriend. I always envied you being able to be open about yourself. But it seems to me you can't let yourself be happy, either. Maybe it runs in the family."

"I'm working on it."

CHAPTER 17

Pulling the Plug

Blake sat in a recliner in the cold room. A nurse brought him a blanket and turned off the overhead lights, leaving only the reading lamp glowing beside the bed. His mother and aunt had gone to a hotel; they looked exhausted from their trip, and he promised he'd phone if anything changed.

The doctor who had seen James earlier opened the door. He was frowning, glanced at a clipboard, and sat beside Blake on the edge of the bed.

"I've got the results of your father's tests, and I'm afraid it's very bad." Blake tried to place the doctor's accent. His words were clipped and hurried. "There is a complete loss of part of his brain; the blood was denied for too long, and now the brain cannot come back. Do you understand? He might live a long time in this condition, but it's improbable that he will ever regain consciousness."

Blake looked at his father. The butterflies appeared on the sheet, lots of them.

The doctor didn't speak. Blake tried to absorb the enormity of what he had said. "Will he have to be on life support forever?"

"He may not, but he will never be like your father again. If we remove the life support now, he won't live through the night. If we keep him alive, his brain may be able to heal enough to control his breathing, but I see from this report that he already suffers from dementia and perhaps Alzheimer's.

That only complicates matters. His brain is already dying, and now the stroke has exacerbated his condition."

"What should I do? Will he ever recognize anyone again?"

"No, I seriously doubt there's any chance of that."

The doctor left the room, and the telephone rang; it was Mary.

"Hi, Mom. I'm hoping you were getting some rest."

"I can't sleep. Why don't I come down there and give you a break to at least let you get some dinner and a cocktail? I know you need it, especially after having to entertain Evelyn this afternoon. I appreciate so much you doing that."

"It wasn't too bad. I think she's hiding a nice person under all that Christian bullshit."

"You remember when I used to believe in some of that myself, then I woke up when my church wouldn't stop telling me my son would go to hell? I told them that's where they could go, and I never went back."

"Thanks, mom. I love you for that."

"And I love you for being the person you are and having the courage to live your life how you need to. You got that from Dad."

"Maybe, but you've got guts, too."

"I'll be there in fifteen minutes."

Blake hung up the phone and went into the little bathroom and washed his face. He used the new toothbrush from the cabinet, then ran his fingers through his hair, stared at himself in the mirror, and asked his reflection questions, but no answers came. There was no sound in the room except the machine pushing air into his father's tired lungs. He sat back in the chair and waited for his mother to come. Soon there were voices outside the door and he heard Mary speaking to the doctor, and after some time she entered the room, took Blake's hand, and cried. She bent over James's sleeping face, kissed him on the forehead, and whispered, "Well, this is it, honey. I wish we could've talked one more time."

She looked at Blake and said, "I know what you're thinking; I don't want you to have to do this."

"Mother?"

"The doctor walked me through it."

"No, Mother, let me do it. Dad asked me to, a long time ago. It feels like murder, but it's what he wants. He's dying already; I want to help him go."

Mary said, "A long time ago?" and sat, holding Blake's hand as he recounted the memory:

"This came to me just now, every word, like it was yesterday; it's like dad is reminding me. I was twenty years old, not long after I came out to you and Dad. We were sitting on the deck of Uncle John's houseboat anchored in the river, holding fishing poles that we knew were useless. We were hopeless at catching anything. Dad said it was the family curse, but it was because we didn't enjoy sitting for hours in the hot sun, hoping to catch something we'd just throw back.

"Dad looked out at the river and moved his pole up and down and said, 'Blake, if I ever get sick and won't be getting well, or if I'm gonna be in bed the rest of my life, or if I lose my mind like most of the men in my family do, I'd like to be let go, if you know what I mean. Dying has got to be better.'

"I understood what he was asking. I said I felt the same way, but I didn't know how anyone could help him with that. It's against the law. They'd consider it murder.

"He said, 'Well, if the time comes, remember what I've said. I won't change my mind.' I said, 'Maybe by then they'll let people help themselves go out.'"

Mary said, "Thank you for that, sweetheart. It makes it easier. He never told me that; I'm glad you're here now." She squeezed his hand and stood. Blake went to James's bedside.

"Show me how."

Mary stood by him, put her hand on his, and said, "This one," and guided his hand toward the machine beside the bed.

She left her hand on Blake's as he flipped the red toggle switch. "We can help him together." She put her arm around him as the noise from the machine stopped.

The sound of rushing air ceased. Mary had ordered there be no alarm, or a flurry of frantic nurses, only the soft sound of his father's last breaths, like the flow of the river against the cattails near the quiet place where he was born. Mary kissed James again, left the room, and closed the door behind her.

Blake needed to cry; he felt it was time to let his tears escape from their prison. He'd never cried in front of his father, not even as a child, until this long trip of memory and goodbye. He kept his eyes on his father's peaceful face and saw a slight smile on his lips. Once again, from beneath the sheet that covered him, came a winged creature: the most beautiful butterfly yet, and the biggest. It didn't look real, as if it were cut from cardboard. Its wings seemed to have been painted by a child with bright colors that swirled and ran into each other, creating even more hues. It flew with graceful movements of its beautiful, stiff wings, slowly and silently, onto Blake's chest, where it disappeared into him. Blake held his breath and was drawn into a whirlwind of colors, and saw in an instant the sum of his father's experiences and hopes, his happiness and his successes, and the awful guilt he carried. He knew his father's memories slept safely with him now until the time they would go to their next keeper. Blake exhaled and felt the relief of his father's welcomed death.

The insects gathered on the window pane. They crawled on the glass until they stopped moving except for their wings fanning the air. Their fragile bodies had formed an outline that filled the window: an enormous heart, a message from James that let Blake know his father was happy, thankful, and loved him.

He napped in the chair, not wanting to leave James alone, and dreamed that he was in a different hospital room. It was old-fashioned and lit by the soft, warm light of incandescent bulbs in antique lamps. A young man lay in one of the four iron beds. A bandage nearly covered his head, and one of his eyes had a patch over it. He lay staring at the ceiling, awake but with a look of resignation on his face, as if he thought his life had ended. Blake could see his memories: baseball games, picnics with a pretty girl, dancing in a darkened gymnasium with lights that twinkled like stars, a big band playing Tommy Dorsey tunes, the feel of a girl's breast under satin, and the taste of apple cider.

The colors of the dream changed to grays, and another man came into the room and stood by the young man's bed. He didn't speak but pulled the covers back from the boy.

"Thank you. I was getting awfully hot."

"I wanted to check on you. We heard about what happened. You got beat up pretty good, but I guess you know that. Everybody at school is pulling for you."

"Do we know each other?"

"You've seen me around."

"But do you know who *I* am? Sometimes I can't remember. Crazy, huh?"

The dream began to fade and dissolve into darkness, but before it disappeared completely, James leaned over the young man and kissed him on the cheek as one kisses an infant, and whispered, "Please forgive me."

Mary opened the door and asked Blake if he was all right, and in his half-sleep state said yes, then fell asleep again. The butterflies had gone.

Morning came. The smog had cleared, and the sun rose over the distant mountains and warmed Blake's face through the clean glass. He went to the window and looked at the sunrise. The California landscape had become the field of his father's birthplace that surrounded the house of his childhood, where he and Chief had run free across acres of green grass and yellow flowers, and shining golden butterflies.

He saw his father standing in the field, with the irregular silhouette of the dark forest behind him on the horizon. Chief stood beside him, nudging his face, and Blake smelled the fresh grass crushed beneath his hooves. James looked at Blake and smiled. He was a young man now, seventeen perhaps. He was dressed in blue jeans and a plaid flannel shirt, a fringed leather jacket, and his best Stetson and cowboy boots, tooled with images of butterflies. He raised his arms until they stretched to each side as if to embrace the world. His palms turned toward the sky, and his face pointed straight up into the sunlight. His smile was nearly as broad as his face. It was the happiest, most joyful image Blake had ever seen, and he knew it was his father's final gift to him.

He looked at his father, so near him in the bed, but so far away, too, and touched his cheek. A warm breeze engulfed him like the wind off the Gulf of Mexico, and he wasn't afraid anymore of what lay ahead, not even his own death.

CHAPTER 18
Southern Comfort

Neither Mary nor Evelyn was in a hurry to return to Florida. Mary decided that James would have wanted her to spend some time in California and see the sights he never took her to see. She and her sister had loved the movies since they were little girls, and Evelyn still had unrequited desires to be an actress. Mary treasured her scrapbook of pages and clippings cut from fan magazines. It was, Blake decided, part of her mourning, as she could pretend James was with her on the tours through the neighborhoods of the stars, and climb the hills to see the Hollywood sign up close.

Mary had introduced Blake to "Rebel Without a Cause" when he was very young, and he bought the video when he got older. James Dean became his first crush, and Mary might have been mortified to know she had also provided him with his first masturbatory fantasies. Blake happily accompanied them to Griffith Park Observatory and the bust of his dead heartthrob.

They rented a car and drove to Baja for a few days. Evelyn was a new woman, now free of the evil ghosts that had ruined her life until now. She said, while sitting on the beach and drinking a Margarita, that she was "Never going back to that fucked up church." Blake spat out his beer, and Mary almost fell out of her beach chair, laughing.

Mary raised her glass and said, "Thank you, Jesus!"

Blake worried about his mother's finances, as she insisted on picking up the tab for everything. She said it was her time to spend some money and have some fun, and Blake had paid for the entire trip with his dad, so he didn't stop her. In truth, he was worried about his own bank account. The trip had put a huge dent in his savings.

A month had passed, and it was time to return home. Evelyn had upgraded their airplane seats to first class; apparently never having children had its financial benefits. She and Mary sat looking out the little windows of the airplane, and Blake was behind them, sipping a vodka and tonic. The cabin was only half full, so Blake placed his leather case in the seat beside him; it held his father's ashes. The flight attendant asked him to put it under his seat, but when he told her what it contained she whispered, "Just belt it in then," and winked and smiled at him.

Movement on the tarmac caught his attention as the luggage cart sped toward the airplane's open cargo door. He watched as the handlers put a cardboard box into the hold; it bore a sticker that signified it was human remains. The lady at the pet crematory gave it to him and said the box would receive better treatment that way. Then she told him that some of the ashes were buried with Audie Murphy. Chief was going home, too.

Blake slept on and off during the flight to Tallahassee, waking occasionally to see Evelyn and his mother speaking to each other, sometimes looking between the seat backs to see if Blake was awake; he'd close his eyes and pretend to be napping.

Blake had reserved a car for their arrival. He'd left his Chevrolet in a parking garage in Los Angeles and hoped it would be okay when he returned. They drove to Evelyn's house to stay for the night. The ashes remained in the car's trunk, along with most of their luggage.

Evelyn made a pitcher of Southern Comfort punch and pimiento cheese sandwiches. They sat on the front porch until the sun was low and the shadows of the Spanish moss reached the green-painted floor; by then, they were tipsy, and Evelyn was more talkative than Blake or his mother had seen her in a long time. She seemed different, as if her dourness had evaporated and she had some happy thoughts for a change. Mary was laughing, too, and Blake wondered if she had accepted her husband's death and was perhaps feeling light and free from the weight of his pain.

At the last light of the sun, its orange and yellow rays touched the oak trees, and Blake looked at the rental car parked in the driveway. A swarm of long-tailed butterflies floated above it, and some landed on the trunk lid for a moment, then disappeared into the fading light and the shadows in the tree branches, soft with resurrection ferns and memories.

James's memorial was in a week. Blake was enjoying the new Evelyn, and she and Mary spent hours reminiscing about their childhood and telling him things they'd kept secret for so many years.

On the morning of the celebration, Evelyn drove them to James's birthplace. Mary gasped as the house came into view; an acre of the meadow surrounding it was mowed, and tables were set up holding flower arrangements and chafing dishes. There was a big barbecue grill made from concrete blocks, and blue smoke billowed from it. The aroma was the scent of home and childhood, and Blake imagined his grandfather bending over the fire, brushing sauce onto the meat with a tiny mop while fending off a gaggle of children trying to steal a piece. James had learned from his father how to cook and had become famous in his town for it, too.

The planter boxes under the windows bloomed with marigolds, and the porch had a fresh coat of paint, as did the white shutters and newly-red front door. Blake and Mary went inside; Evelyn stayed behind. Blake looked out to the meadow and saw her standing with a woman about her age, and they hugged each other the way old friends do.

People were arriving in cars filled with food and folding

chairs. Someone had brought a settee and put it in the little living room, along with some other pieces. The long dining table was in place, and women were already in the kitchen filling platters with food. They had arrived before dawn to cook cornbread, okra, yellow squash, jello salad, loaves of homemade bread, baked chickens and baked beans, and meat that Blake feared was raccoon. They brought deserts that almost covered the dining table; iced brownies, key lime and pecan pie, banana pudding, German chocolate cake and peach and blueberry cobbler, plus an enormous platter of tea cakes. Blake took one, tasted it, and as the powdered sugar melted into his tongue, knew Mrs. Hoggett had brought them.

All the effort these people had gone to, and what they'd accomplished so quickly, made Blake feel inadequate. Why hadn't he become more like them? They were his people, after all, his tribe. He felt some questions about his father were being answered; how he had the knowledge to do almost anything that needed to be done, and how he never seemed afraid of not succeeding. In his youth, there'd been no alternative. To survive and prosper, one had to catch life and subdue it. There was no option to fail; that was not a consideration.

It was almost noon, and the field had filled with pickup trucks, some new, some battered, and station wagons, and several Cadillacs, Buick Electras, and Lincoln Continentals. A crowd of people surrounded the house and tables; the porch was full of them balancing plates piled with food, sitting in metal folding chairs they'd borrowed from church. Someone set up a card table and used it as a bar; bourbon was passed all around, and a toast was made in James's memory.

Mary held Blake's hand, got teary-eyed, and said, "James would have loved this. He loved a party, and everyone loved him being there." There were many hugs and conversations about childhoods, families, deaths, babies, and James, who was loved by all. Many had come from hours away. Some were still living down the dirt road, the one that James had seen Chief disappear on, taken from him when his heart was still soft and easy to break. Blake thought of the vision he'd seen of his dad and Chief standing in the field, and the joy on his father's face, and hoped he was with his horse, and happy. He wanted to believe that. He would not apologize to himself for feeling now that life can go on, no matter what, and that maybe there was happiness waiting for him, too.

Dinner was over, and it was time to go to the river to toss the ashes into its dark currents. It was Mary's wish that they be put there since she knew it was James's favorite place in the world, and the woods it flowed through had been where he became a man, and fell in love with life. She wondered if the place where they stood on the bank of the river, holding the mixture of James's and Chief's ashes, had been the spot where they had camped, and where a cottonmouth moccasin had tried to take his life.

Blake and Mary filled their hands with the gray sand and let it flow between their fingers into the river, downstream toward the Gulf of Mexico. No one spoke, but the sound of tears being shed drifted into the trees and across the iced tea colored water. Mrs. Hoggett was crying louder than the others, and Blake wondered if there was another story to be told, one that a butterfly held, not yet shared, but he didn't care.

There was a woman on the bank upstream from the rest of the group. Blake watched her toss a bouquet tied with a blue satin ribbon into the water. It floated with the current past him, close enough that he saw the flowers were blue irises.

The walk back to the house would take a few minutes. Mary joined Evelyn, and Blake held back, waiting for the woman who'd thrown the flowers to catch up with him. She walked carefully, stepping over roots and stones in the pathway, and when she reached him, held out her hand and said, "Hello. I'm Marguerite."

Blake guessed her age as a youthful mid-forties. She pushed her straight blond hair away from her face and looked at him.

When he saw her eyes, he sucked in his breath; they were an amazing color of blue, like glacial ice, and he saw his father looking back at him. He couldn't speak and waited for her to say more.

"I don't know how to tell you this. I'm afraid it will shock you, and perhaps hurt."

"Judging by your eyes and your flowers, I think I already know."

"The flowers were from Margaret, my mother. She found my whereabouts when I was a young adult, old enough to understand, and we kept in touch. Your father was my father, too. I didn't know him. It's a long story. But she left instructions in her will on how to contact you after she and James were gone, and to tell you the truth. She also left her estate to me. So... surprise!"

CHAPTER 19

A Gift for the Blessed

Blake looked into her eyes, trying to absorb what she was telling him, and pondering its possible effects.

"So you're my sister?"

"Well, half-sister anyway. Don't be angry with your father. He never knew. That's what my mother wanted."

"Half-sister is good. It's great, in fact. I'll take it." Blake smiled and wondered what her life had been like.

"Your mother... I don't know her or how she'll react to this. She may be happier not knowing."

"I think she'll be okay with it. She's a very understanding person nowadays." He was still staring into her eyes. She cocked her head and looked at him with a quizzical smile. Blake said, "I'm sorry, I'm in shock. And I can't believe how much you look like my father — our father."

They returned to the house. Evelyn watched them go up on the porch and sit next to his mother. Blake said something to the few people that remained there, and one by one they rose and kissed or hugged Mary, then went into the yard; a game of horseshoes had begun.

It intrigued Evelyn that Blake seemed to be asking the others to leave their places. He and Marguerite sat across from Mary and were speaking to her. Evelyn was too far away to hear but watched as Mary hung on the words of the young woman, and after a few moments, stood and put her fingers to her lips, shook her head, turned to Blake and spoke to him, then went into the house. Blake followed her. Marguerite stayed alone on the porch.

It seemed quite a long time before Blake came back and sat with Marguerite. His mother appeared, dried her eyes with a tissue, and approached the woman. She bent close to her, said something into her ear, some private words even Blake couldn't hear, and the women embraced. After a while, they were laughing.

They sat and talked into the late afternoon, and Marguerite told her story. Her English was perfect; better than most of the people there. Her accent was cultured Parisian. She told them how Margaret had found she was pregnant when she was dating James. "She was so confused. Her boyfriend was in the Army and was far away, and she knew James would have to leave, too, and maybe get killed in the war. In those days, an illegitimate child would ruin your reputation for life, and the child would suffer, as well. And she was a Catholic. But she wanted to have the baby because it was James's, so she did, and gave the baby up to a couple in New Orleans who moved back to Paris after the war was over. I was raised there. That's why I speak French."

Mary touched Marguerite's hand and looked into her beautiful eyes. "Looking at you is like seeing James. I'm glad you got a chance at a good life. I think Margaret did a brave thing. And as far as I'm concerned, you're my daughter now, too."

Mary looked at Blake and said, "James and I had a daughter. Her name was Margaret, too. Isn't that something? Quite a coincidence, isn't it, Blake?"

Blake shrugged and showed his palms.

"We lost her. She died. She was still young but not well and never had a chance at happiness."

Marguerite said, "I'm so sorry for you."

Mary smiled at her and said, "Thank you for coming to us. I hope it wasn't too frightening."

Marguerite tried to smile, but her look was melancholy.

"You've both made it a wonderful experience, and I'm sad to go.

"I hope we stay in touch now. There are thousands of stories to tell, I'm sure. And, just so you know, I have two sons and a daughter in France. They're wonderful children. Talented and so beautiful. It's obvious there are good genes in your family. My daughter is studying ballet and hopes to become a professional dancer; my oldest son is entering the Sorbonne to study medicine. There are times I wish James could have known his grandchildren."

Blake said, "And the youngest? My half-nephew? Is that correct?" He smiled and shook his head in happy disbelief.

"I think so. I was never good at figuring out family titles. He is my special child. I love them equally, of course, but there's something magical about Benoit. He seems to be clairvoyant and an empath of sorts. He says he sees things no one else does, and I believe him. Sometimes his interests get a little tiring. He's been crazy about insects since he was tiny, especially butterflies, and I spend a fortune having the ones he catches mounted and framed," she laughed. "I am worried about his future, though. I think he may be interested in only boys, if you know what I mean, and the world is a hard place for people like that."

Mary said, "If I can remember my high school French, Benoit means 'blessed', correct? Lovely name."

"That's right. I felt he was blessed when he was still in my womb."

"My son is blessed also, if you know what *I* mean. And the world can be hard for anyone, not just the blessed."

Marguerite looked at Blake and said, "I'm not surprised you're blessed. You're too good-looking not to be, at least just a little."

"That's what Dad said when I told him."

Marguerite winked at him. "I know. I'm a little blessed myself, in the way our father was, and I think you are, too; you are doubly blessed"

Blake put his hand on his chest, felt the heavy silver

necklace there, and smiled. There came the sudden stab of longing in his heart again, and he knew it would be a long time before it went away. He missed Seth's gentle presence and sweet understanding. He'd longed for it since the day Seth left him, and sometimes at night, alone in his bed, could still feel Seth's arm holding him, grounding him to the Earth, comforting him, and leading him back to reality when he needed it the most. He wished he were here beside him now.

Evelyn joined her family on the porch, and Mary began the long explanation of Marguerite's presence and the history of what brought her there that day. They stayed there after nightfall, drinking and laughing, their confusion and judgment erased by their sudden closeness, helped by the warm effects of Jack Daniels and Coke.

The summer brings thunderstorms on a regular schedule in the part of the world that they occupied, and one was brewing to the west of them. A wall of wind surprised them with its strength, and soon rain was blowing sideways, chasing them into the front room to look out of the big sash windows at the furious beauty of the storm. Great booms of thunder shook the house, and bright lightning flashes lit their faces. Their eyes were wide with awe and delight at nature providing such magnificent entertainment. If they'd been sober, they might have cowered in a bedroom until the storm was over. Whiskey and the comfort of each other had given them the courage to stand and watch the wind blow the trees, and the rain obscure the landscape, and not be afraid.

The storm moved on and peace returned, but the power was out. Evelyn found a kerosene lamp, and she and Mary went through the house to check for damage.

Blake yelled to them, "I think we might've had a little tornado," and went out onto the porch, breathing the rain-clean air that smelled of wet soil and broken pine limbs. His foot hit something on the porch floor, and he knelt to find it in the dark. A silent flash of lightning from the departing storm illuminated the object lying there. It was out of place and inexplicable.

Marguerite came onto the porch just as Blake stood up with the thing in his hands. It was a wooden pole, almost weightless, and the net fabric attached to one end looked old, but not torn; a child's butterfly net.

He smiled at Marguerite and said, "A present for your blessed son, the butterfly collector, from the best grandfather he could ask for."

"I know he will love it. He's told me recently that he's stopped putting them to death to display them. He said now the butterflies bring thoughts of other people to him."

Blake said,"We have to talk more about this. I would love to visit your family sometime. Benoit is blessed in more ways than you imagine."

The old beds had been made before they arrived, and Blake was glad to have a room to himself. He slept soundly until the voices of Evelyn and her friend came through the thin wall from the bedroom next to his. He smiled and put his pillow over his head, and went to sleep again.

The next morning, Mary was awake and making coffee when Blake went to the kitchen. She handed him an empty cup, and as he filled it said, "I'm glad you're up early. I need to talk to you before you leave."

"Okay," Blake said, smiling at her, hoping this would not be one of Mary's mother-son chats. He was far too old for any of that.

"Let's sit on the porch. It's a beautiful morning. Sun's just coming up." Blake followed his mother to the porch swing, and they sat and watched the sun rising behind the oaks, looking like fire in the distance beyond the dark silhouette of the trees. The sky was filled with birds and huge white clouds, tinged orange and pink by the dawn.

Blake sipped his coffee and said, "Okay, let's talk. I hope it's something good."

Mary said, "You know your father was talented with money, judging by the way you lived coming up. We never wanted for anything. We were rich in a lot of ways, but we never talked about money. James was like that; money was a secret thing, and to show off what you had was bad taste, and could be dangerous. It's the Southern way, you know. If people know you have money somewhere, they'll try to take it from you. I think it's a holdover from the Civil War and the carpetbaggers."

Blake said, "It's not a bad way to be. It's nobody's business what you have in the bank, I guess," he laughed. "I've never had that problem."

Mary smiled. "That's what your dad used to say. Even I never knew for sure how we were set; I saw the real estate and the stores, and the new cars, and your trips to Europe, and I just assumed we were doing pretty well. I trusted your dad with everything, and he never disappointed me. That's the way marriage was back then."

Mary paused and took Blake's hand. That worried him; she looked as if she were going to divulge some terrible secret.

"Your father had more money than anyone imagined. Now that he's gone, it will come to me. But eventually it will be yours."

"Jesus, Mother, how much is there?"

"Well, there's enough to provide for generations if it's not squandered. And the sale of the real estate will make us very rich if that's what you want to do with it."

"What *I* want to do?"

"I don't want the burden of all that money. I wouldn't be comfortable dealing with it. So, I've decided to leave some of it where it is and live off the interest. Trust me, there's enough. As far as the rest, I'm giving it all to you. The houses, the rental apartments, the land, the stocks... that's what your father wanted, after I die, but I don't think it's fair that you have to wait for that. So, son, you're going to be a very wealthy man. There's one piece of land that developers are already lining up to buy; it alone is worth millions. I'm sure you won't have to work anymore if you don't want to. Or at least now you can work at something you love."

Blake was holding his cup near his lips. It froze there the moment he'd heard his whole life had changed, and it would be incredible.

Finally, he said, "Holy shit!"

His mother kissed him on the cheek and said, "I know you won't let it change you. You're too level-headed for that. But I hope you have fun with it; do all the things you've always wanted. That's what your dad had in mind for you. That's why he worked so hard; not so much for me, but for his children."

"And," she said, "believe it or not, he left a nice gift for Evelyn. I think he always liked her, despite how she was with him." She looked at the sky, now bright and pristine. "She can start the life she's always wanted, with the person she needs."

"So you know about her?"

"Oh, heavens, yes. For years, everyone knew; no one cared but her. Poor Evelyn, we've had so much love waiting to give her, but her judgmental ways and her religion wouldn't let her accept herself. We felt that telling her we knew might destroy her. She already believed she was going to hell. Her world was all wrapped up in her church and the Bible; it was her security. She would have fallen apart if she lost that."

"Are you ever going to tell her?"

"We had a chat last night, after you went to bed. She's so relieved. She cried, she was so happy."

Marguerite joined them on the porch. "I have to leave in a few minutes, and I wanted to say goodbye. Thank you for putting me up last night. I hope you'll keep in touch. Come visit us in Paris, or maybe in the south of France for the summer. We have a cottage there. It would be so nice if you could be friends with my children and my husband. They're all wonderful people."

Blake said, "Don't forget the butterfly net. It came a long way, from another time, I think."

"I will give it to my blessed one, along with James's picture your mother gave me." She looked down and said, "I would love it if I could be part of my family."

Blake said, "You are already. It's wonderful to have a sister again."

Marguerite went inside to get her luggage. Before going to help her, Blake said to his mother, "What about Marguerite? She's his daughter, after all."

"That will be taken care of; James would have wanted that. She and her kids are in for a pleasant surprise. Which reminds me of one more thing you should know."

"I don't think I can handle all this in one lump."

"You'll be glad I told you. When James's attorney went through Dad's papers, he found a box of cancelled checks. He pulled out the ones that seemed odd and gave them to me."

She handed the bundle to Blake. He took the rubber band from around it and glanced through them, and saw they were all made out to an assisted living facility in Tallahassee he'd heard of that was only for the wealthy.

"So, what does this mean? Was he paying ahead for you, or the both of you? Two thousand a month?"

"See the notation at the bottom?"

Blake read it. It was a man's name, one he had heard but couldn't remember why it meant something to him. He looked at Mary, unsure of what to ask her.

"That's the name of the boy who was almost beaten to death. You know what I'm talking about."

"Yes, I remember, but no one ever said what happened to him. Dad never talked about it."

"The young man had been so brain-damaged that he could never live a normal life again. His family wasn't well-off, so your dad made sure that he got into the best facility in this part of the state. He stayed there for thirty years until he died at forty-seven. Your father sent a check every month for all those years. The parents never knew where the money came from; no one did. But even with doing that, he never got over his guilt."

CHAPTER 20

Turbulence

The man sitting next to him on the airplane chatted his way across the continent. Even in the worst turbulence Blake had ever experienced, he kept talking, as if the threat of sudden, violent death in the Rocky Mountains below had no effect on him, and didn't distract him from telling his life story. Blake willed him to shut up, but he looked at Blake and continued. He had a dark, vacuous expression in his eyes. Blake ordered another cocktail and put his sleep mask on, and slid deeper into the sensuousness of his leather seat. The man, unfazed by Blake's inattention, kept speaking.

Blake dreamed he was a little boy in a room full of old men. He was naked, and the men sat around him in rickety ladder-back chairs, and stared at his body like vultures in trees waiting for their dinner to die. Blake cried; he was cold and afraid, and wondered where his mother was, and why she hadn't come to take him out of this room. The only light that entered was from a tiny window high on the concrete block wall, and the floor was hard and dusty, and painfully cold on his bare feet. One man took off his pants and began masturbating. A voice from behind him said, "Go ahead. Do it." The man came toward him, smiling, and put his hand on Blake's head.

Blake awoke, shaken and horrified by his dream. The airplane was descending through the parchment-colored smog over Los Angeles. A flight attendant stopped at his seat, looked at his crotch to check his seat belt, smiled and nodded, then glanced at the passenger next to Blake. When he saw the startled look on the flight attendant's face, Blake turned to the man and saw he was pushing a hypodermic needle into his tattooed arm. The man looked up at the attendant, chuckled, and said, "Blood sugar's up."

The plane touched the runway. Blake felt disgusted; a dream hangover. He let his seatmate go ahead of him in the queue of passengers, and as he retrieved his suitcase from above his seat, turned to Blake and said, "Nice talking to you." The man's face had been in his dream, and Blake felt nausea forcing its way toward his throat. As he walked to the exit, Blake saw a flurry of brown moths above the man's head.

Blake reached the end of the jetway. A group of uniformed people stood around the man lying on the floor of the waiting room, his eyes open and staring at the ceiling, and his body twitching. The secrets he had tried to force into Blake were flying around him; black ones, mud-brown and bile green, bruise purple and blood red. They flew to the ceiling of the dismal space and disappeared. They seemed to know that Blake wouldn't accept them, that the memories they carried were too vile and evil for anyone to allow them into their mind.

Blake wanted Seth; he needed him to pull him out of the unknown and the darkness again. He wondered if he'd ever be able to navigate the curse he'd been given. Seth said it was a gift. Blake felt it was more akin to contracting genital herpes.

The Impala was still in the parking garage, safe and sound. The fee was horrendous, but he was relieved that it was all right, since Los Angeles, to him, was a hotbed of crime, and car theft was a favorite. He was glad his car was too old to be desirable to thieves. He checked into a hotel near the airport for the night to rest from his trip and process the possibilities of the direction his life had taken.

The hotel bed was luxurious, but held memories of love-making strangers, and sad people full of hate for their partners, couples with children still bright with future dreams, and old men who were feeling alive for the last time. Their butterflies still lived in the room, unable to leave, but anxious to fly out into the world, even though unsure of their destinations. Blake went to the big, double-glazed window that overlooked the vast parking lot and, farther away, the strings of lights and endless pavement that had led so many to heartache and defeat. He was anxious to leave the city in the morning.

He opened the window; the sound of the traffic and jet engines assaulted him as he watched the creatures flutter out into the night to search for their next hosts, eager to unburden themselves of their cargo.

He couldn't sleep. It was late on the East Coast, but his mind was churning with so many thoughts that sleep was going to be impossible for a while. He ordered a hamburger and a carafe of vodka and tonic, turned on the television, and tried to get comfortable in the enormous bed.

An old black and white movie was playing, and it drew him into its sweet naiveté. Thoughts of Seth made the bed too big and cold; his gut writhed with longing and regret that he'd spoken harsh words to him. He knew Seth was right, but when he was younger, he would fall in love with almost anyone he'd slept with, at least more than once. He knew his dad would tell him to grow up and get on with his life; someone else would come along, but right now, in this bed, he wanted Seth.

Somewhere up the coast highway, in a little town that harbored wanderers and creators of beauty, Seth stood on a stage. It was a small room as venues go, but he liked the intimacy, the perfect lighting, and the appreciative patrons who were never rude.

Madame Psyche felt older, but she was as beautiful as ever, and her talent could still bring people to their feet and even make them cry if that's what she wanted. She sang now, and didn't lip sync anymore, for she'd found her own voice was more effective than miming dead stars.

It hadn't been very long since she'd been with Blake, but sometimes it felt like years. She sang a song and hoped he would hear it some day and think of her. There was no reason for him to; they'd never heard it together, and she didn't know if he knew the song, but to her, it was theirs.

She sang "I'll Be Seeing You", and thought of Blake sitting in a cafe in Montmartre, looking into her eyes as if there was nothing else in the world but her. No butterflies, no heroin, no unspoken, secret pasts. She finished the song and cried on stage, and for a moment everyone understood Billie Holiday's pain. The audience was silent, except for a few sympathetic sniffs.

Blake, in his bleak, starkly decorated room in the dream city of Los Angeles, was still awake and watching the ancient movie he'd chosen. The muffled sound of jet airplanes combined with the hum of the air conditioner. His half-closed eyes opened a bit when someone on the television started singing a sad, old song about Paris and lost love. He didn't recognize the voice or the performer, but he drifted into sleep with the soundtrack carrying him into a vision of a cafe on a gray cobblestone street. He smelled the seductive aroma of French roast and tasted red wine on his tongue. A beautiful man, blonde and youthful, smiled sweetly, and he thought his heart would break.

He embraced Seth, drew him close to kiss him, warm and deep and long, and the people surrounding them applauded and began singing, "I'll Be Seeing You".

CHAPTER 21

A Turquoise Triumph

Morning came, and Blake turned on the television. It was comforting to have coffee in bed and watch the news the way he did at home. He still had hopes that someday, someone cuddled beside him would offer to fill his cup.

He wasn't interested in the local broadcast, but it caught his attention when the newscaster said, "A confessed child predator, and perhaps murderer, on the run for three years, was arrested yesterday at Los Angeles International as he exited his flight. LAPD had received a tip that the man would be on the plane; strangely enough, the tip is rumored to have come from the suspect himself. The man collapsed from a self-administered overdose of an undetermined substance as the police put him in handcuffs, and he is hospitalized in critical condition. More on this at eleven." He hit the off button on the remote. He knew the rest of the story.

Blake wanted to rid himself of his gift. He wanted peace and to be loved. The butterflies were beautiful, but not the dark, winged things that followed the evil people. He was learning the variety of his visions; they weren't always pretty, and they weren't all welcome.

And now, a new burden had presented itself. Was he meant to warn others when he saw danger? If a disaster loomed, would there be butterflies and moths around those about to die? Would murderers seek him out to unburden themselves as death approached, like a last-minute confessional to a priest who would choose to be ignorant of their hideous corruption?

He didn't want warnings or terrible dreams, and had tired of butterflies carrying other people's pains and unforgiven sins. He craved love in the warm safety of his bed, a lovely cocoon protecting him from random strangers with stories to tell, or people he loved who had secrets that haunted them. Perhaps it could be a place he could share with someone else. His gift had taken him too far away from the beauty he needed like water and sun. It had to stop.

He needed Seth to help him navigate out of this darkness; he would know why this new, dark, horrible vision had assaulted him.

The next morning, Blake said a sad goodbye to his aging Chevrolet at a classic car dealership, then drove north on Highway 1 in a totally restored, turquoise Triumph TR4. He wasn't sure where he was going, but knew he wanted to stand under giant trees and breathe oxygen straight from their ancient limbs, and drive until he found his destiny, free from his past, and open to the future.

He felt drawn to a place that he hadn't seen, but had imagined; a place of clarity and perhaps happiness. And as he drove and looked out at the Pacific Ocean and the rocky shore and the windblown trees, still standing despite decades of storms, he was enthralled with the beauty of it and the promise of more of the same ahead.

He shouted into the salt air and pine needle shadows, and a hum of ecstasy built in his chest, "Goddammit, I'm fucking rich, and I'm gonna be happy! Thank you, Daddy!" When he said it, he wished his dad were beside him in the car, and wondered if his father had driven this highway so long ago, on his way to San Francisco and his first drag show.

The car's canvas top was down, and his hair whipped his face into numbness, and the sun on it felt like a kiss from a handsome, horny man. The sound of the engine brought him a memory of an Englishman driving the car through a jewel-green countryside, perhaps traveling to a secret tryst with the owner of the grey castle in the distance. He saw the man sitting next to him in the passenger seat of the car that had once upon a time belonged to him. He smiled and released a butterfly to live in Blake's mind, then whispered, "He was a Lord, and he was fucking gorgeous, like you are!"

Blake saw through the man's eyes and said, "Yes, he was!"

He stopped for lunch in a California-perfect town at the ocean's edge. There was an upscale cafe; the decor was a faded hippie style, begging to be discovered by some Bon Appétit food queen. That, of course, would be its demise, but in this moment Blake savored his time there and ate salty, metallic oysters, fragrant herbed bread and spaghetti carbonara.

He enjoyed gourmet food, but only allowed himself to indulge in it on special occasions. It seemed a wasteful extravagance to him. But now he would make up for all the meals not eaten, and all the places unseen, and the wine he hadn't tasted. He had held back long enough.

Mary said he wouldn't let the money change him, but he knew she was secretly afraid he might become someone she didn't want him to be; she loved who he was. She didn't know that he liked who he was, too, and was just realizing that. He felt the feeling bloom in his mind. It was a new joy for him to reject the guilt, fear, and shame he'd carried throughout his childhood and beyond.

He understood Evelyn; it isn't only religion that inflicts self-hate. Sometimes it springs from inside a person, like the seed of an ugly weed planted long ago by some vile, unthinking stranger, or a teacher of children, or a poem on the boy's room wall.

He hopped into the sports car, over the door, then sped away from the restaurant and yelled again into the clear air, a scream of pure joy and freedom and love for life, and, finally, for himself.

He hoped Mary would let herself enjoy some of life's pleasures, too; the things she hadn't allowed herself to indulge in. She might have done so if she'd known of the wealth sitting in her husband's secret accounts. Blake decided that, when he settled down again, he would redecorate her house to be the home she'd always wanted. He would ask her to send him all the clippings from *House Beautiful* and *Southern Living* she'd saved through the years, and he'd take it from there, starting with her new curtains.

He continued his drive north. The scenery seemed to be more breathtaking at every turn, and he sensed he was in sweet danger of never going back. California, the home of Yosemite, redwoods, and snow-topped mountains, free-thinkers and rainbow flags, and San Francisco, the gay capital of America. He headed toward it and would arrive after a night in the fairy tale village of Carmel-By-The-Sea, where he sat on the sand and watched the sun set into the dark Pacific, and daydreamed, and made plans.

He took his wallet from his jeans and pulled out Seth's business card. He hadn't looked at it since Seth had given it to him, and he saw that a heart had been drawn by his name. Blake felt the familiar stab of longing, and decided that a phone call wouldn't hurt. After all, that's why Seth gave it to him. And damn, he wanted to hear his voice. He would call, now, before he changed his mind.

He began to run down the pristine beach, clutching the card in his fist to protect it and to perhaps feel Seth's energy in it. In the near darkness, he stumbled on something buried in the sand and fell forward, instinctively spreading his fingers on the way down to soften the fall. Seth's card escaped his hand and was caught by the offshore wind and sailed away toward the dark ocean waves. Blake tried to go after it, but a flash of searing pain in his knee kept him from running, and he could only watch it disappear into the approaching mist and pale, setting sun.

He awoke too early. His first thought was of the lost card, but he brushed his anger and frustration aside and let the excitement return to him that he thought had gone. The pain in his knee had been soothed by the ice pack he'd used, and the Tylenol he'd taken, and he ignored what little pain was still there. He telephoned Mary to tell her his location; she was glad to hear from him and had been worried. Then he phoned his office and spoke to Amanda. She'd been running his studio while he was away. She was a valuable, hard-working helper and a very talented artist, and his clients loved her work and her genial personality. He wanted to do something nice to thank her for all she did to make his business run, and for making his time off possible. They chatted for a while; she said work had been busy, but not overwhelming.

"You need to look for another artist and an assistant," he said and waited for her to react.

"Is there something I don't know? Did you land a big client? Or are you letting me go?" She laughed, knowing that Blake would be lost without her, and he knew it.

"No, it's to help you out. You can't do it alone."

"What are you talking about? Don't tell me you're dying or going to jail."

"None of the above. It's just that I'm done with what I've been doing for fifteen years. I want you to take over. I'm giving you all my clients and some money to set you up in an office. Oh, hell, keep the office. I'm giving you the house, and I'll float you for as long as it takes to get going on your own. You already know everything, anyway."

"What the fuck, Blake? I can't believe it — what's happened? You are too good to me. I think I'm going to cry. I can't thank you enough. But how can I work without you here to inspire me?"

"You'll be fine, and we'll keep in touch. I'll tell you all about it later. I know you've always wanted your own business. I'm off for San Francisco. Have a drink tonight in that Lesbian hangout of yours, and buy a round for the bar, on me. Charge it to the business. I'll miss working with you, too. Love you, later."

"Blake, be careful there. There's stuff in the news..."

"I know. I will be."

He hung up the phone and tried not to panic; he'd always avoided burning bridges, but as soon as he looked at the road map to plot his route to San Francisco, his fear vanished, and he threw his clothes into his suitcase and ran down the staircase to his car.

"There's no turning back now, Dorothy!" he said aloud, and a man coming up the stairs laughed and smiled as he passed.

The man said, "Good luck, Judy!"

He drove to the beach and walked the sand, hoping the card might still be there, visible in the soft morning light.

Probably half way to Hawai'i by now, he thought, and headed toward the highway.

CHAPTER 22

Catharsis on Highway 1

The fog moved slowly from the sea onto the city as he drove into the thick of it. He found a hotel in the Castro neighborhood, showered and went shopping, and bought an outfit that would make him blend with the locals. Even though he often received compliments about his body, he'd never been proud of it, and he never wore tight jeans. But now, the mirror showed him he should.

"That's a fine ass you've got, young man," he said, and left to join the river of men walking the streets: hungry hopefuls thirsty for liquor and love, anxious to dance under the shiny ball and get high on poppers. Some brushed by him and turned back to admire his new jeans, sometimes whistling or flashing a thumbs- up sign. He couldn't help smiling.

He was in heaven. "Keep your head," he thought to himself. He knew what lurked in the streets and inside many of the people who walked there. There were butterflies everywhere, some flitting aimlessly, some landing on the shoulders and backs of the men, waiting their turn, preparing themselves for the work ahead. They made him fear what might be coming.

One place seemed the busiest. He squeezed his way between half-dressed men, felt a few gropes of his denim-encased ass, and walked through the front door. A sign read "Welcome to Uncle Sam's. Play Nice. Don't Forget to Salute!"

This was the club he had come to see. A thrill ran

through his body as he opened the doors, knowing that his father had passed through them before him so many years ago. A bronze plaque shone just inside the entrance, polished from the thousands of hands that had rubbed it, remembering a fallen comrade. It read:

"In Memory of Our Own Angela Mercy,
Miss San Francisco Queen of 1944,
Taken From Us In Her 27th Year
Mere Steps from This Place
By The Hands of Evil, Hateful Demons.
Your Talent, Beauty, and Kindness
Will Live In Our Hearts Forever."

It was early, and the club was almost empty. He sat at the bar and ordered a drink from the shirtless bartender, who said, "You must be new here. First time in Frisco?"

"Does it show? Now I'm embarrassed. I don't want to look like a tourist."

"I wouldn't worry about it. Half the people in here are tourists hoping to get lucky." He looked Blake up and down and said, "You won't have a bit of trouble."

"My father was here during World War Two. He told me about the drag queen who got killed."

"Murdered by some straight, drunk rednecks from Texas. She was walking home after her performance. My boyfriend has newspaper clippings. So, your dad is gay?"

"No," Blake laughed, "I don't think so! He was here with some of his soldier friends to see a drag show. He just passed away, and I want to visit places he'd been to back then, to feel closer to him, I suppose."

The bartender mixed another drink for Blake. "That's sweet. I wasn't fond of my dad. He liked to beat me up on a regular basis after he found out I was queer."

"I'm so sorry. Guess I was lucky to have a dad like mine."

"What was his name? We've got a lot of pictures on the

wall of people that used to come here. This club has been in business since the thirties. Most of the pictures have names on them. You should check them out."

"His name was James Eaton. I'll look around."

The man said, "Hang on. This is crazy. Look at this." He took a small picture from the wall behind him. "The owner had this framed, so everyone would remember." He handed it to Blake.

It was a check, paid to the order of the club. He noticed that the amount line was in a different handwriting than the others. Then he saw a familiar hand on the signature line: *James R. Eaton*.

"Was this for his bar tab? He must've had quite a night."

"No, your dad paid for the plaque by the door. He sent that check after Angela was murdered. He'd ordered the thing from a shop down the street, but we had to pick it up, so he sent us a blank check to pay for it. He trusted us that much. There was a note with it; it's kept in the office safe. The owner treasures it. I know it by heart. It says 'From a straight soldier who loved the show and hates any fucker that would harm any of you. This country is fighting for you, too. Please remember that. Love, James Eaton.' That thing must have cost him a month's soldier's pay."

Blake smiled and wished his father were there. "That's my dad."

Blake left the club before the show began. On his way to the hotel, he ignored the glances from the men; there could be danger there, and even if not, he wanted to stay away from anything that could alter his mood. His mind was rested and clear, and a one-night stand would change that. He had a hunch that something good was coming, and it might be tainted by the lingering touches of a stranger.

He spent two weeks walking the streets, riding the cable cars, and dining on the waterfront. He hiked the Bridge, toured Alcatraz, ate a gourmet meal every night, wrote postcards to his mother and Evelyn, and saw a performance of *Il Trovatore*.

Now, he was glad to leave San Francisco. In only two weeks, it seemed to have changed. It felt sad and dirty and on the edge of disaster, and the people looked joyless and afraid; rumors of the coming plague had spread.

The highway beckoned; he didn't want to stay in the city for another minute. He left his hotel in the evening and drove into the coming darkness. The sun was setting on his left, and redwood forests and the entire continent of North America stretched away on his right.

In the twilight, on the black highway near the ocean, lights flashed red and blue. He slowed and approached them. The road was blocked. He stopped close to the scene and saw a long object on the asphalt, covered by a blanket, and a white dog running in circles, sniffing it and crying, like frightened animals do. A semi- truck had stopped not far ahead. Its hazard lights were on, and a man crouched next to it and held his face in his hands.

A policeman came to Blake's window and told him to turn around. There was a detour a half mile back; they were putting up the signs.

"What happened, officer?"

"The truck driver said he saw a girl run into the road to catch her dog. She was walking him, and he slipped his collar; he couldn't stop in time."

Blake turned around and parked in a pullout down the road. The sun had left a thin glow of red lingering on the horizon. He got out and lit a cigarette, and the horror began to overtake him, beginning from just under his heart and pushing its way up toward his mouth, now open and gulping in the salt air but unable to make a sound.

His legs buckled and the pain from the sharp gravel assaulted his knees. He covered his ears to muffle the roar of the speeding truck in his mind, and his eyes filled with tears of acid, as if they could blind him to the movie playing in his head, the one he'd seen so many times but couldn't erase.

The scream erupted from him like a putrid projectile of

emotions; an ancient, angry mass that had tormented him for years. It had begun its way up moments before, when he saw the lifeless girl on the hard pavement, and now it was ready to burst from him. It came, long and loud, and his throat burned as it clawed its way up toward the air. The captive creature made of foul words and old poisons and hate and self-imposed guilt was fighting its way out at last.

"Why did you do that to me? I loved you. I always protected you. Why me? Why do I have to see it over and over for the rest of my life? You fucking bitch, I wanted to save you! I tried; I couldn't move fast enough—I was afraid. Did you want me to die with you? I wanted to live! Now leave me alone—you got what you wanted. Please let me go. Goddammit, I want to be happy!"

Blake's sobs flew out of him, over the waves, and toward the darkness. He vomited bile into the brush, wiped his lips on his sleeve, and looked at the ground through a blur of tears. In the failing light, he saw the hideous creature lying there, convulsing as it died.

"Dammit, Margaret, I miss you. We tried to love you; we wanted to—why wouldn't you let us? I'm sorry you were sick. We just didn't know."

He stood for a while, then wiped the last drops of his anger and sorrow from his mouth. The light was nearly gone, but he could see a moth, large and pale green, far from its habitat, land softly on his damp shirt sleeve. It unfurled its tongue and tasted his fermented sadness, caressed his hand with its delicate legs, and flew away, just like that.

CHAPTER 23

Mahler in the Dark

The TR4 seemed to need speed, like a racehorse that's been kept in its stall for too long. Blake turned on the radio and tuned to a station playing Mahler's Second Symphony, his favorite. He pulled off the road and sat on the hood of the car listening to genius coming from the speakers, and smoked a cigarette. The piece had just begun. He'd seen it performed years ago in the Albert Hall, and it lasted for an hour and a half.

Blake drove onto the highway. He decided that in ninety minutes, when the symphony ended, he would stop, and wherever that was, is where he would stay, at least for the night, or maybe linger there forever.

The dark comforted him. He stopped again and closed the canvas top. The music moved on without him, urging him to catch up. He drove fast and didn't dream; he was driving far from the unrelenting memories and into his future.

The symphony was showing him his past. The movements seemed to illustrate his pains and his joys, but especially his losses. He realized then he'd never truly been himself, but also that now life was offering him a chance to redeem that squandered time.

The melody crescendoed toward its ending; the voices of the choir became the spirits of the universe. Blake was always overcome by this part, so he stopped to listen in front of a little cafe in the center of a village. It was cloaked in darkness, but the lights from the windows made it look happy and welcoming. The end of the symphony came, and as it did every time he heard it, made him believe temporarily in an afterlife. He sat in the tight leather seat and smiled, and wondered, could he be healing?

He put his forehead on the steering wheel, closed his eyes, and said, "Dad, I miss you. Seth, I need you."

After some time passed he dried his face, wrangled his hair into presentability, found his wallet under the seat, and went intothe cafe.

It could have been a hundred years old and was lit by gas flames and mirrors. He sat at the carved mahogany bar and imagined it had come from a steamer that had wrecked on the rocks below the town. Mozart played on the sound system, and the few late-night patrons were young and dressed in formal clothes from an earlier era. It looked like a night at a Rocky Horror Picture Show screening; the fans waited quietly for the main event, and Blake wondered what that would be.

He ordered a bourbon and Coke. He was staring down at his glass when, from the corner of his eye, he saw an attractive, heavily made-up woman approach the counter and lean over it. A red ostrich feather curled from her hat and blocked her view. Long white gloves covered her arms. She said to the bartender, "Give me a shot of vodka. I can't do another show without it. I'm kind of off tonight."

It was the voice he longed to hear again, the one that soothed him, brought him back to himself, and taught him how to handle his gift. He knew her perfume. He raised his head to look at her reflection in the mirror behind the bar, then turned and saw her standing only a few stools over.

"Seth?"

The woman froze with the vodka suspended in the air halfway to her mouth. She paused for what seemed an eternity. Finally, she put the shot glass to her lips, swallowed, then slowly and dramatically, in silent screen fashion, looked down at Blake. Her green-shadowed eyes were full of passion, and she threw her head back and became Norma Desmond at the end of the movie, and spoke like an angry diva.

"Well, it fucking took you long enough!"

"I didn't know where I was going."

"Yes, you did. You got here, Blake."

Blake's eyes pleaded. He said, "Have you forgiven me?"

"Of course. Have you forgiven me?"

"I forgave you a hundred times, all the way up the coast, then I realized there was nothing to forgive."

"I'm glad you figured that out. But why do you look so sad?"

Blake reached for Seth's hand. "Please help me. I think I'm happy, and it scares me."

Seth laughed so loudly that everyone in the room looked at them. "I'll help, but it's going to take a long time. You're really fucked up."

"Dad died, but I guess you know that."

"The moment it happened. I'm sorry.

"He's happy. It was awesome."

"He's still around you."

"So, can I stay at your place?"

"Of course, it's just upstairs, but I'll have to kick my boyfriend out first."

Blake's smile disappeared.

"Just kidding!"

"You're still a bastard. Let me get my things from the car. I need to freshen up."

"Take your time. I need to change; I have a show in half an hour. Go to the back there. I'm at the top of the stairs. It's not much, but it's home."

"Go do your show, but promise you'll come back afterward."

"Always, baby, always."

In the sweet moments that Seth and Blake talked and held on to each other and tried to hide their elation from the customers, the intercity coach stopped at the gas station down the block. A couple of passengers got out and walked away from it. One went south toward the houses, and the other went north toward the shops and the one bar on the street. Blake had parked near it and was gathering his things to take upstairs. He was bending down to get his bag from the trunk when he heard a voice from behind him.

"Hey, you, Blake!"

Blake turned to face the man.

"You mother-fucking slime. Psyche's next."

Things happened so quickly that later he couldn't remember seeing the pistol in Mark's white-gloved hand, or the smirk on his powdered face, or the pearls around his neck. But he remembered the boom of the gun echoing in the street, and the terrible pain in his chest, and falling into the dark.

He lost consciousness, and when he awoke, a ring of people surrounded him. Seth knelt by him, held his hand, and smiled. He said, "You're fine, sweetie, everything's fine. I love you."

A police car, one of the town's two, parked nearby. In one of them, Mark's face stared out from the back seat. An ambulance arrived and took Blake to the little clinic a few blocks from the cafe. Someone said, "We just want to make sure you're okay. You took quite a hit to the chest. Thank god you wore that necklace; it saved your life. You must've turned away right before it hit you; it was a glancing blow. It's kind of a miracle."

Seth said, "A bitch on the tour told him where I got off the bus. It was probably Holly Trinity, you know, from Las Cruces. Mark was coming for me, but finding you here must have made his day. I'm so sorry."

Seth held the silver piece so Blake could see it. "It's wounded, but I think it'll live. You can still read the inscription from the jeweler: 'May This Keep You Safe From Harm.'"

CHAPTER 24

Saving a Boy

They awoke in Seth's room above the cafe. The feel of Seth's body, the smoothness of his skin, the firm muscles beneath it, and the natural perfume of it, all felt like home to Blake, as if he'd always lived there.

Seth had turned on the news and brought coffee to the bed. They lay, sipping coffee with one hand, and cupping the other's private parts with the other. Blake's hand was growing numb, so he removed it from Seth's erection. "Could you rub some of that stuff on my chest, please? It still hurts."

Seth took his hand from Blake's body. "Sure, babe. It's going to be sore for a while. I'm so sorry that happened to you. I feel kind of responsible."

"Why? You saved my life. I mean, if you hadn't given me that necklace..."

"And if you weren't wearing it, which, by the way, I thought was incredibly sweet."

He massaged the prescription into Blake's skin, starting over his heart.

"I left Pernod in LA after our gig was over. He wouldn't give up the shit. I tried to help him, I really did. It hurt to leave him, but I had to. She was threatening me; I was afraid of her. He showed up at the tour bus, but they wouldn't let her on, so she stood on the sidewalk and shot me a bird. She had a gun. I should have called the police, but the bus was on its way."

Blake put his hand on Seth's and followed its travel around his chest. "Just as long as we don't have to worry about him anymore"

"Oh, he'll be in prison a long time, I hope. Maybe they'll get him off the shit. Or even better, someone will kill him. In any event, he'll have lots of boyfriends."

Seth laid his head on Blake's chest.

"It's okay, Seth. I'm here and everything's wonderful."

"If he had killed you, I would've died inside. I'm so fucking glad you're here now and I can hear your heart beating."

"Tell me you won't run this time."

"Only to where you are. You know, I never slept with Pernod again. I didn't want to. She wasn't the same person, and I knew I was in love with you. I hadn't been with anyone until last night. I just wanted to be with myself for a change."

"That makes me happy, I have to admit. I'm kind of a prude, you know."

"That's one thing I like about you. I won't have to worry about catching something."

Blake gave him a look of reproach.

"Sorry. I guess that's in poor taste these days." He laughed and did a spot-on Streisand impression, "But at least I'll know where you are nights."

Blake cringed. A voice inside him said, "Just stay quiet, Blake." He was quick to confess things most people thought were only normal human behaviors and not worthy of guilt.

"Well, now you don't have to go anywhere else." Blake took the cup from Seth's hand, nuzzled the back of his neck, and said, "Do you know your skin smells like apples?"

Seth said, "So eat me," and soon they awoke the desires of the night before.

Later, still in bed, Blake held Seth in his arms and said, "There's something I need to talk about."

"I think I know, but go ahead."

"It's about my dad. Alzheimer's runs in my family.

Chances are…"

Seth propped himself on one elbow and kissed Blake. "Oh, that. Don't worry. If that comes, I'll have your back. I'll be there."

"You mean that? It could be many years from now."

"I want this many years from now. I hope you do, too. I've waited for you for so long, maybe thousands of years. I won't let you go." He fondled Blake's testicles. "I'm hanging on to these."

Blake felt that worry leave him. It floated to the ceiling and grew smaller until it was almost invisible. He said, "What did you think I was going to say?"

"Never mind, babe."

"There's one more thing that happened I want to tell you about. I need your help to understand it."

"Stop feeling guilty. You made no promises to me."

"Fuck, you know about that? I don't know, Seth. Being with you might put a crimp in my promiscuity."

"Like that ever happened."

"No, it's about a man on the plane." Blake told the story and described the terrible images in his dream and the arrest.

"God, that's a big one. I think it was about the little boy, not the pervert. Maybe the child was trying to reach you. The answer will probably come to you. Just give it time." Seth kissed Blake's cheek. "Forget about it for now. Let's just stay naked today; I want to feast my eyes on your perfect body."

"I'd love to, but I want to see the town, and people here might frown on that. What is this place, anyway, and why are you still here?"

"The town told me to stay. I was on the tour bus passing through on the way to a gig in Portland, and we stopped for lunch. I didn't get back on the bus. Simple as that. You're gonna love it here; I do. I never want to leave. And I want to quit performing. It's time."

"What do you want to do instead? Hair?"

"Well, now don't laugh, but I'm a pretty good painter.

Not of houses, but of artwork. I got my degree in painting and fine art; I'm not just a pretty face."

The television newscaster caught Blake's attention. He was talking about the kidnapping and rape of the young boy that Blake had become in his dream; his whereabouts were unknown, and a body hadn't been found. Before he died, the rapist insisted he hadn't killed the boy. The monster said he left the youngster at the crime scene, naked, hungry, and bleeding, but alive. He was supposed to kill him, but the kid was kind of special, and he couldn't bring himself to do it. He was going west, anyway, to commit suicide in his hometown of LA. He had planned to jump from the Hollywood sign but chose poison at the last minute.

Seth looked at Blake, took his face in his hands, and said, "Close your eyes. Become that little boy again. Go back to your dream. Pick up where you left off."

Blake sat up on the bed. He let his mind spiral backward into the dingy, dim room and saw the man coming toward him.

"Don't make me go through this, Seth."

"You have to, for the kid. If he could survive it, you will, too."

"And if he didn't?"

"Just do it."

The pain was unbearable. Blake screamed for his mother and tried to push the man away, and cried and screamed again, and then lost consciousness.

"Stay there. Keep your eyes closed… Does the boy wake up?"

"He's opened his eyes. The men have gone. It hurts to move, but I'm at the door now. I can't open it; it's locked. I'm pushing a chair up to the window, and I see a forest outside. My clothes are in the corner and I put them on. I get the window open and pull myself up, and climb through it. The forest is beautiful; very tall trees that smell nice, like Christmas. I'm crying for my mother again."

"Can you see where you are? Is there a road, or a house?"

"I'm walking, and now I can see a road. I'm afraid to go there. The men may still be there. There's a noise, and I look down and a big rattlesnake is curled up near my feet and I run away toward the road. There's a sign. I can't pronounce it. It's like Ouch something. I see a trailer, and the door is opening, and one of the men is coming outside. I'm running away now, back into the forest."

"Can you talk to him, Blake? Can you tell him to hide in the forest?"

"I'm trying. He's there now; only trees and nothing else around him. I'm telling him to lie down and hide, and don't move a muscle. Seth, I know that place. It's a state park near Tallahassee. My dad used to take me there."

Seth called the Tallahassee police. An officer answered, and Seth gave the receiver to Blake.

"When you get out there, look for vultures circling. That's where the boy is. He'll still be there. No, I'm not kidding. Please, go there now. Hurry! Look for the vultures."

"Baby, you may have found a new purpose in life."

"I don't want it!"

"Tough shit. It's yours now, Blake. And for god's sake, smile! You should be happy. You just saved a little boy's life."

They went out for breakfast. The main street was lined with turn-of-the-century gingerbread houses and brick buildings, all of them with window boxes full of cascading flowers. As they neared the part of the street closest to the ocean, Blake saw a red brick, three-story building, well preserved for its age, with a small For Sale sign on the plate-glass window. Blake asked Seth to remember the phone number for him. He wasn't as good at that as he used to be.

"I guess not…" Seth said. "Did you ever call the salon number I gave you?"

"Short, sad story. I'll tell you sometime."

At breakfast in a cafe with a view of the ocean, Blake used the pay phone across the street. Seth watched him hang up the receiver and look toward the old building. He looked so handsome, his blond hair blowing seductively in the breeze from the ocean, his jeans tight and showing a provocative bulge, his posture straight and confident, something Seth hadn't noticed before. He pictured his future with this beautiful man. Perhaps, finally, he'd done something right.

Blake sat down at the table and smiled. "How'd you like a place to hang your pictures?"

"I don't understand. I haven't painted anything in ten years."

"Well, you'd better get busy."

The next morning, while having their coffee, the police phoned to tell Blake they'd found the child; he'd been in the woods for days, but was alive. They expected him to be covered in insect bites and starving, but he wasn't hungry, and there were no bites. It had been the way Blake predicted; they followed some circling vultures, and the boy was below them. He feared the big, ugly birds were going to eat him, and there was a rattlesnake on a log, watching him the whole time.

"The weird thing is," the policeman's voice became a whisper, "the kid said that the day he escaped, a man came out of the forest and showed him where there was a freshwater spring, and told him he could eat the soft ends of palmetto fronds, and eat partridge berries, too, and rub beauty berry leaves on his skin to keep the bugs away. He said the man came back the day you called us and talked to him until we showed up. The man told him stories about his little boy and his horse. Oh, and he had eyes the color of the sky. He left him there and went back into the woods just before we found him. We arrested three guys in a trailer. The boy identified them as the other perverts."

In a week, Blake closed on the building, and the renovations began. Workmen were hired, drawings made, and Blake morphed into the interior designer he'd always had tucked away inside him.

Seth insisted on continuing to do his performances in the cafe. He'd collected a following and realized the love of show business hadn't left him yet. Blake created a studio for him in the back of the gallery, and during the day, he'd paint there. He was working on a huge canvas, a surprise gift for Blake.

When he finished the piece, he put a satin blindfold on Blake and led him into the studio, and with a "ta-da", removed it. Blake gasped, and his eyes locked on the painting. He didn't speak for a while, only stared at the picture, shaking his head in amazement. Apart from the subject, Blake realized in that moment that Seth was a genius.

The painting was the scene Blake saw from the hospital window on the morning after his father died. Seth had painted it exactly as it had been; his father was a young man, standing in a field that looked like the place where he'd grown up, his arms held straight out from his sides, with Chief behind him, nuzzling his neck. James's face aimed at the sky, his palms turned upward, catching the sunlight. His face portrayed all the joy Blake had seen in him; the release, and beauty of his death, and perhaps his new existence.

Blake put his arm around Seth's shoulders. "That's the most beautiful thing I've ever seen. How did you know?"

"You sort of told me. You were dreaming, and I saw it, too."

Blake had to let go. He pulled Seth to him and kissed him, and the tears came, inevitable and unstoppable.

"You haven't cried for your dad yet, have you?"

"I fucking love you so much."

"Man, if you knew how much I've wanted to hear that."

Six months went by, and the top floor of the building became a minimalist apartment, soon to be featured in *California Design Magazine*; the second floor was an art gallery named Mary Eaton Fine Art. Mary had dreamed of being an artist or a writer, but had a family instead. Blake phoned all over to find paintings by his father's first love, Margaret. They were now very expensive and collectible. They were the first show in the gallery. Soon, Seth would produce enough art for his premier exhibition.

The ground floor housed a cafe and bar. Seth had agreed to perform there on special occasions, like the opening of his first show. The space was now a near-replica of an old bar in a town in Louisiana, and was named the Wild Iris Cafe. There were always vases on the table holding Louisiana irises. The cafe would become famous for its "Mrs. Hoggett's Tea Cakes", and every month, Ruby-Ann received a check for the kind use of her special recipe. Soon, the cookies were being sold throughout the state of California, in the best supermarkets, and Mrs. Hoggett was going to become a rich old lady. Blake designed the logo: a cute cartoon pig in a teacup.

It was Blake's rule that every evening at the cafe's closing time, the staff and any customers remaining had to sing "Let Me Call You Sweetheart". Blake had the lyrics printed on the backs of the menus but told no one why.

The opening was a success; Seth performed in drag, sang his old love song about Paris, "I'll Be Seeing You", and sold one of his paintings. The painting named *James in the Field* hung on the back wall of the room, and there were many offers to buy it. Of course, Seth refused them, saying, "That belongs to my lover." People from San Francisco and Los Angeles had driven up to attend, thanks to Blake's marketing expertise, and the write-ups in the press would be glowing. The business was bringing tourists to town, and the other business owners were thrilled.

The next-to-best part of the evening was the surprise appearance of Marguerite and her husband; they'd come from Paris for the event. With them was Benoit, their youngest. He and Blake became friends instantly, and, even with the language difference, seemed to have known each other for all of the boy's life.

Even Mary and Evelyn attended the opening. Evelyn brought her partner; she was a lovely lady who had shed the chains of her earlier, cult-led influences, and was happy at last. The couple spoke of moving to California because they wanted to "truly breathe free". Florida, they said, was becoming stifling, and too conservative.

Mary brought a gift for the boy's new apartment and Blake couldn't wait to open it. Seth stood on his little stage and held the heavy package, and Blake stepped forward to unwrap it. The lights dimmed, and only the spotlight on the stage remained illuminated. Blake, with a dramatic flourish, tore the paper from the object to the sound of breaths drawn and polite applause. It was a brass wall sculpture of a horse's head, with a long mane of curling, flowing metal rods of gold, formed into the shape of the wind blowing through it as if the horse had just run free from a barn in Arizona, or into a Texas tornado, or away from a river in Florida, carrying a loved one to a place that could save him.

CHAPTER 25

So Fucking Happy

The crowd thinned a bit. A few people left, laughing as they went, and held souvenir brass figurines of a rearing stallion. Blake was glad the evening was ending. He never liked crowds unless they were of friends or family. People had a way of draining his energy and making him crave a quiet and slow conversation with someone he loved. That had always been hard to find. He could talk to his father like that, telling stories of the family, or their town, or themselves, slowly, bringing life to their past and making the future seem as wonderful. There could be long pauses between words; time to look at the sunset or have a long drink from a glass of bourbon and Coke, and no one ever felt awkward about the silence.

Blake went out to the salt air and the elusive, lemon fragrance of the redwood trees on the hills, and stood on the sidewalk and lit a cigarette, the first one in weeks. He inhaled the welcomed smoke and watched the people inside the cafe in the mellow amber light hug each other as they prepared to go, or ask the bartender for a refill. Seth worked the room, making sure the hangers-on had fun.

He imagined James with Mary. The music got sweeter, and he watched them dance a slow waltz from a time before Blake's existence.

Aunt Evelyn and her lover did a very respectable ballroom routine, together in public for the first time. They had met at an audition for *Auntie Mame* at their local playhouse, and Evelyn landed the title role. There was a standing ovation, and Evelyn had never felt so loved.

Marguerite, her husband, and Benoit held hands and whirled around the room. Blake wondered what Margaret would think of her daughter and her grandchild. Marguerite began pulling others into the wheel until it grew and filled the space. Men were moving tables to create more room for the growing ring of dancers. Later, Blake would swear to Seth he'd seen Margaret dancing with her family.

Blake stood on the sidewalk, thinking of the years he had stayed outside the circle, denying himself the closeness that it might have brought him, feeling he didn't belong and wishing he could be more like them. All those years they had loved him more than he'd loved himself. Some thought he was conceited or imagined he was above them, but the truth was he'd been ashamed and afraid to tell them who he was.

From the darkness of the empty street, a young boy and a woman came toward him, holding hands and smiling. The boy broke away from his mother and ran up to Blake, hugged him around his legs, looked up at him and said, "Thank you for saving me."

The boy's mother came closer, looked at Blake with tears in her eyes, and said, "Seth told us how to find you. Bless you for bringing my son back to me!"

Blake said, "Oh, I am blessed already."

Seth came out and put his arms around Blake. "I've got a present for you, too." He took a whistle from his pocket and blew it long and loud, and in a few moments Blake heard a sound coming from the dark. It was familiar, but out of place.

A horse and rider stepped into the light. He was golden, with a beautiful silky mane, and glistened in the glow from the cafe windows. The rider ordered the horse to rear high into the night, block out the stars, then trot to Blake and nudge his face with his own. Blake couldn't speak.

"It's Cochise, honey. Happy opening."

"What?"

"Bill Watson, the horse trainer, passed away, and I got the owner to part with Cochise. He gave me a great deal, and I got three huge painting commissions and I wanted something awesome for you tonight. He's staying at the stables in the hills up there, and I think that's where you'll be building that cabin you always wanted. Just a hunch."

Someone put "We Are Family" on the turntable, and the circle broke and became a conga line that flowed out through the big doors into the street. Someone pulled Blake into it, and pushed him to the front of the line and showed him the steps. His father's voice whispered, "Get in the dance while you can!" Seth found him and encircled his waist with his arms and guided him to the middle of the street.

The dancers formed a circle again, and it got smaller and tighter and soon Blake stood in the center, with arms holding him like a mother cuddling her child. Blake was laughing so hard he cried, and realized in those heady moments that he hadn't felt such joy since he was a child in a field, with a wise rattlesnake protecting him, and the memories of his ancestors floating above with the sunlight shining through their wings.

He looked around and saw faces smiling at him, and his mother blew him a kiss and shouted, "We love you, Blake!"

He stood up as tall as he could. The dancers backed away, and he looked up into the darkness, his arms stretched out from his shoulders, his palms open to the night sky. Seth ran to him, afraid something was wrong. He clutched his waist to hold him down and keep him from flying away.

Blake looked at the faces in the little crowd and yelled, "Dammit! I love you too! And I'm so fucking happy!"

They stood in the street for a long time. The crowd drifted away to their cars and guest houses, and Cochise was returned to the hills. Seth still held Blake around the waist, standing behind him on tiptoe, with his chin resting in the crook of Blake's neck. The sky had the slightest tinge of sapphire daylight; the sun was still low and hidden behind the hills. Blake removed his denim jacket, laid it on the curb, and sat, pulled Seth down, and put his arms around him. Seth sniffed, and Blake pulled him even closer and kissed him. "I know. I've never been this happy, either."

Seth wiped the tears from his eyes. "Are you tired?"

"Not at all. And not the least bit sleepy."

"I have an idea. Let's drive up into the hills toward the sunrise and look at a piece of land I found. It's all redwoods. It would be perfect for your cabin."

"*Our* cabin?" Blake said.

"Yes, *ours*."

They locked the cafe doors and walked the gray street to Blake's car. He stopped and said, "Shit, I forgot my car keys."

Seth hugged him and whispered into his ear, "They're in your hand."

The top of the rising sun shone through the trees and looked like a forest fire, and the air was getting warmer; the day ahead promised to be beautiful. Blake dropped the convertible top and they stripped off their shirts and drove, smiling, toward the expanding light.

End

EPILOGUE

Blake willed the tract of land near his hometown to Benoit, and then, to keep it safe from developers, asked the Governor to give the land protected status as a wildlife refuge. The land will remain pristine forever, and the Governor named it the *James Eaton Forest Preserve*.

Blake and Seth often visit there. Both enjoy talking to the visitors and sharing the wood's secrets.

Seth invented a female character, a Seminole Indian Princess, and dressed in traditional native costume reads the story of a horse named Chief to the children.

Blake designed and had constructed a butterfly conservatory near the visitor's center. The building is a smaller version of James's childhood home, but has glass walls and window boxes filled with native wildflowers for the butterflies. People love to stroll the flower-perfumed pathways and exclaim about the beauty of the insects that float so close to their hands.

Every three hours, there is a showing in the conservatory of an old film entitled "Storm in the Desert".

If Blake notices a youngster who is blessed, he invites the child and their parents into the forest and teaches them how to call the vultures from above the straight pine trees, out of the open sky, to land nearby and wait.

In the years to come, Blake and Seth will be married in the conservatory, both in their hearts and in the eyes of the government. Butterflies will caress them and fly in circles above their heads, and carry the memory of that moment to be saved for much later when their children receive it as a last gift from their fathers.

Just inside the doorway to the conservatory hangs a giclée copy of *James in the Field*.

A monument stands by the entrance to the park. Its base is a pedestal of coquina rock on which is a bronze plaque bearing an inscription carved into the shiny metal:

"Welcome to the
James Eaton Wildlife Sanctuary,
Made Possible by His Vision and Gift.
Tread Softly and Speak Kindly to the Living Things,
Especially the Butterflies;
They Are the Keepers of Our Memories."

Above the words is the likeness of a beautiful horse standing on its hind legs as if jumping toward the sky. His mane waves in the wind behind him, and in the distance curves the snake-like shape of a tornado. Beneath the horse there is one word: *Chief*.

NOTES

Diderot's *Encyclopédie* cites butterflies as a symbol for the soul. A Roman sculpture depicts a butterfly exiting the mouth of a dead man, representing the Roman belief that the soul leaves through the mouth. The ancient Greek word for "butterfly" is ψυχή (psȳchē), which primarily means "soul" or "mind".

In some cultures, butterflies symbolize rebirth. In others, the butterfly is a symbol of being transgender, because of the transformation from caterpillar to winged adult.

In the Philippines, a lingering black butterfly or moth in the house is believed to be the spirit of a recently deceased loved one.